I SAW ZOMBIES EATING SANTA CLAUS

I SAW
ZOMBIES
EATING
SANTA
CLAUS

A *Breathers* Christmas Carol

S. G. BROWNE

G
GALLERY BOOKS

New York London Toronto Sydney New Delhi

Gallery Books
A Division of Simon & Schuster, Inc.
1230 Avenue of the Americas
New York, NY 10020

First Gallery Books hardcover edition October 2012

GALLERY BOOKS and colophon are registered trademarks of Simon & Schuster, Inc.

For information about special discounts for bulk purchases, please contact Simon & Schuster Special Sales at 1-866-506-1949 or business@simonandschuster.com.

The Simon & Schuster Speakers Bureau can bring authors to your live event. For more information or to book an event contact the Simon & Schuster Speakers Bureau at 1-866-248-3049 or visit our website at at www.simonspeakers.com.

Designed by Jaime Putorti

Manufactured in the United States of America

10   9   8   7   6   5   4   3   2   1

Library of Congress Cataloging-in-Publication Data is available.

ISBN 978-1-5011-0915-7
ISBN 978-1-4767-0873-7 (ebook)

For my readers

I wake up on the ground in darkness.

Faint artificial light filters up into the night sky, silhouetting the trees below me and creating a soft, ambient glow that's reflected off the falling snow, which doesn't make any sense because the last thing I remember I was inside the research facility. So it's a little disorienting to discover I'm flat on my back on a hillside.

That and I hear somebody humming "Jingle Bells."

When I sit up, something rolls off my chest and down the hill, coming to rest against a mound of earth with a *thud.* It's some kind of heavy black metal cylinder. I get to my feet and walk down to retrieve it. At first I think it's a flashlight but when I pick it up, I realize it's a stun baton. And the mound of earth isn't a mound of earth but a decomposing corpse.

I'm in the body farm.

Half a dozen human bodies in various stages of decay are laid out on the hillside around me—some of them fresh, some of them mummified, some of them sinking in upon themselves, doing what corpses do best: decaying in their own, fragrant way.

I look down at the nearest one, which looks like it's pregnant. Since the corpse is male, I'm guessing it's not a miracle of medical science but is instead in the late stages of bloat.

When the human body dies, the bacteria that live in the stomach continue to feed. Though instead of eating the food we've consumed, they start eating away at us and excrete gas, which builds up in our abdominal cavities until eventually something gives way. Usually the intestines but sometimes the torso. Either way, it's not something you want to occur on a first date.

Not speaking from firsthand experience, but sometimes it happens.

I look around at the corpse-infested hillside and try to remember how I got here and what happened to me, but my powers of recollection aren't lending a hand. Or even a finger. That probably has something to do with the fact that my head feels like someone hit me with a sledgehammer. I look down at the stun baton and think maybe I got clocked with it when I notice my shirt is soaked in blood.

I don't know if it's my blood or someone else's but I'm hoping for what's behind Door Number Two. However, since it's dark out and I'm feeling a little disoriented, it takes me a moment before I realize that I'm neither bleeding nor drenched in someone else's blood but am wearing a Santa Claus suit.

I'm not exactly built like your traditional St. Nick.

You wouldn't call me chubby or plump and I don't have anything that shakes like a bowl full of jelly. I'm a leaner version of Santa. More like the AFTER picture than the BEFORE.

However, I am sporting an authentic beard, not one of those fake, synthetic jobs. We're talking thick and bushy, which is what happens when you don't shave for twelve months and your hair turns white. I'm no Edmund Gwenn from *Miracle on 34th Street,* but I look as much like Kris Kringle as your average Salvation Army Santa.

While I remember where I got the suit and why I'm wearing it, I still don't have any idea how I ended up in the body farm or what happened to everyone else. The last thing I remember, we were all inside the research facility, singing Christmas carols and handing out candy canes and spreading holiday cheer.

I'm guessing things got a little out of hand.

I look around the body farm surrounded by the darkness and the falling snow, caught for a moment inside my own little warped snow globe, trying to piece together what happened and why I'm out here all alone. I'm about to walk down the path to the front gate when I notice the humming again. Only instead of "Jingle Bells," they've switched to "Santa Claus Is Comin' to Town."

The humming is coming from beyond the trees above me, so I walk up the hill, past a man wearing a maggot merkin and a woman melting out on to the ground around her like the Wicked Witch of the West, until I come to a small clearing on the hillside. A couple of Santas and a naked guy walk around among a dozen or so corpses, most of which are naked themselves and staked down with U-shaped rebar around their wrists and ankles. All except for one, which is neither naked nor staked down and isn't a corpse yet, but that's just a matter of time.

He's wearing a Santa outfit, just like me. The major difference between us is that he's getting eaten alive by a pair of elves.

The elves sit on either side of him, dressed all in green with fur-trimmed red hats and green rubber surgical gloves, humming "Santa Claus Is Comin' to Town" in perfect harmony with one another as they share an evening snack. When the elves see me, they stop humming and look up with matching smiles.

"Hey Andy," they say in unison.

MY NAME IS Andy Warner and I'm a zombie.

That's not something you ever really expect to admit. Alcoholism, sex addiction, gambling problems? Sure. They just come with the territory of the human condition. But you just never plan to wake up one day with a cannula inserted in your carotid artery and your body cavities packed with autopsy gel.

It's a big adjustment coming back from the dead. Kind of like going through puberty, only the acne and the smell never completely go away. But most Breathers just can't seem to understand. They act like we can do something about the way we are. Like we did this to ourselves on purpose. As if we had some kind of choice.

It's not like there's a twelve-step program for being a zombie. You can't just go to a bunch of meetings and get a sponsor and cure yourself of undeath. Once you reanimate from the dead, you've pretty much crossed a line and there's no going back.

As a whole, zombies tend to have trouble accepting their new reality. That's something a friend of mine used to say. Accept your reality. While that's good in theory and a healthy philosophy to live by, putting it into practice is a lot harder than you'd think—especially when your reality involves having to worry about bloat, maggot infestations, and getting dismembered by fraternity pledges.

And you thought *you* had problems.

When I say I'm a zombie, I'm not talking about the typical mindless, shambling ghouls you'll find on the screen at your local cineplex. Most movie zombies are brain-dead monsters that lack any spark of humanity and are unrelenting in their single-minded purpose to devour anyone in their path.

Kind of like politicians, only with less corporate funding.

Real zombies aren't Romero wannabes. We're just normal, sentient, reanimated corpses who are gradually decomposing and who could use some serious therapy. No moaning and groaning. No cracking open skulls with our teeth. None of that ridiculous Hollywood crap.

Except for the eating of human flesh. Turns out they got that part right.

The elf on the left takes a bite of Breather and points at my face while the other one says, "Ouch."

I reach up and discover I have a dime-sized wound on my forehead. At first I'm not sure what it is or why I can fit my pinkie inside of it, until I reach around to the back of my head and find the exit wound.

That explains my headache.

I hate getting shot in the head. Talk about misinformation. It's just a movie, people. A plot device for a script so your main character can avoid getting eaten and move on to the next scene. The truth is, shooting a zombie in the head just makes a big mess. That and it's kind of hard to cover up with makeup.

I need some Advil. And I could probably use some gauze and Neosporin. Maybe a hoodie to keep any flies from getting curious.

"Is he the one who shot me?" I ask the elves.

They look at me and nod together, then go back to eating the Breather.

"Oooo," he says. "Eee aaa oooooo."

When you're getting eaten alive, you tend to speak mainly in vowels.

I recognize the Breather's face but his name escapes me. While you can't kill a zombie with a head shot, there's a definite adverse impact on mental acuity. After all, when your gray matter explodes out the back of your skull, you're probably not going to win any spelling bees.

The good news is, zombies don't need their whole

brain in order to function. We don't even need most of it. Considering the majority of Breathers get through their lives barely using their brains at all probably has something to do with that. But I'm still a little fuzzy about everything. It's all a little surreal, in a holly-jolly-zombie-Christmas kind of way.

If you've never woken up in a body farm wearing a Santa suit with your brains blown out the back of your skull, then you probably wouldn't understand.

THREE DAYS AGO

ONE

I'm strapped down to a table in one of the examination rooms with my head immobilized, naked except for a pair of blue hospital booties on my feet. Sometimes they let me wear a surgical gown but more often than not I'm naked, which doesn't do much to nurture my sense of dignity. But when you're a lab rat being experimented on in the name of medical research, dignity isn't a high priority.

"Was the subject disinfected?" says a lab technician, inserting a catheter into my penis.

"No," says another one. "But I'll take care of it when we're done setting up."

A couple of lab techs wearing scrubs and surgical masks are prepping me for my latest test. I'm the subject in question. And by *disinfected,* they mean sprayed from head to toe with Lysol. Every time I'm disinfected, it reminds me of my mother spraying me with Glade neutralizer fragrance whenever I would come into the house from the wine cellar. That was before I started to regenerate. Before I stopped decomposing. Before I ate both my mother and my father.

Sometimes zombie/parent relationships can get complicated.

The lab techs continue setting up whatever test they have planned for me today, although "today" is relative. Days don't really have much meaning when you spend your existence in windowless rooms getting stabbed and shot and electrocuted, subjected to impact tests and toxicity tests and experiments involving tissue regeneration.

Right now I have electrodes attached to the side of my head, the wires running to a machine with gauges and meters and recording equipment on a cart next to me. Maybe if I were a doctor or a scientist or a *Jeopardy!* champion I would know what the contraption is called, but I was a property manager in my former existence. Before I died. Before I reanimated. Before I led a push for zombie rights that culminated in a New Year's Eve bloodbath and eventually landed me a permanent stay at this research facility inside the Oregon Health and Science University in Portland.

I'm thinking it would have been a little more helpful had I been something other than a property manager, something that might come in a little handier for someone who's been involuntarily donated to medical science and held against his will. Like a personal trainer at a gym. Or an escape artist. Or MacGyver. Then all I'd need is some baking soda, some hydrogen peroxide, and a hot water bottle, and I could get the hell out of here.

Although I don't have any real concept of time since

I never see the sunset or the moonrise or feel the changing of the seasons, I'm aware from listening to conversations and seeing the decorations in the hallways that it's the week before Christmas, which means I've been here for nearly a year.

Time flies when you're getting electrocuted and infected with syphilis.

"Goggles," says one of the lab techs.

They both don their goggles and the next moment I'm being sprayed down with Lysol. I'd prefer they use Pine-Sol or Simple Green or something that doesn't make me smell like a freshly cleaned toilet, but I don't get a vote.

At least they're not disinfecting me with Comet.

There are other zombies at the research facility with me, so I'm not the only one being poked and prodded and tested in the name of research. But I've been here longer than anyone else and as far as I know, none of them was ever interviewed by Oprah.

While I realize I'm no longer a celebrity, and that to the researchers and interns and handlers I'm just another nonhuman, zombie lab rat with a number instead of a name, it would be nice to know what they're doing with me and why I haven't been sent off to a composting facility. The only thing I've been able to determine is that they're studying me and the other zombies to find out why we reanimate and how we're able to heal and reverse the process of decomposition by consuming human flesh.

Not that they're feeding me John and Jane Does. I

haven't tasted Breather since last New Year's. And technically I haven't eaten anything since they brought me here. After all, it's kind of tough to chew when your mouth has been sewn shut with industrial-strength thread.

The only way I receive any sustenance is through a feeding tube that's permanently inserted into my stomach. Not because I need to consume the recommended daily allowance of whole grains and fruits and vegetables. Zombies aren't known for their omnivorous diets. But whatever they're feeding me is keeping me from decomposing.

The lab techs just finish spraying me down when today's zombie researcher walks into the room. He's dressed in a white lab coat with a particle mask covering half of his face and safety goggles perched atop his head. The ID badge attached to the pocket on his lab coat identifies him as Robert Rudolph, but most everyone at the research facility calls him Bob.

Bob and I are old friends. And when I say "friends," I mean Bob has conducted numerous experiments on me during the past twelve months, including most of the electrocutions, stabbings, and ballistic impact tests. So our friendship isn't exactly based on a solid foundation of trust and mutual respect.

Bob speaks with the lab techs to verify that everything is all set and that I've been properly prepped, then he dismisses them from the room. After they leave he walks over, removes his particle mask, and looks down at me.

"So how are we feeling today, RC-1854?"

That's me. The RC stands for Reanimated Corpse. I presume the number 1854 indicates how many test subjects came before me. They never refer to any of us as zombies or by our names here at the Research Lab Hotel. And we don't get complimentary wireless Internet or chocolate mints left on our pillows or four-hundred-thread-count, 100 percent combed cotton Frette linens.

I look at Bob without responding. I'd like to tell him how I'm feeling—which is a combination of cold, uncomfortable, and ambivalent—but with my mouth sewn shut, it kind of makes it difficult for me to share my thoughts.

Bob looks down at me with a smile plastered on his face, like he's a game show host and I'm the contestant who's made it to the final round. There's something about Bob that reminds me of my old therapist, Ted, who would often sit there in his chair and stare at me with his own fake, plastic smile as I wrote down on my dry-erase board how I felt about being a zombie. That was before I decided I didn't need his help anymore. Before I began to find my purpose. Before I ate him.

Which is one way to ensure doctor/patient confidentiality.

"Do you know what we have planned for you today?" says Bob, still wearing his disingenuous smile.

No, I think. I didn't get the memo. Whatever it is they have planned, I'm guessing it's not something I really want to put in my scrapbook of memories.

"We're going to start a new type of therapy today."

Bob picks up a needle and syringe from the tray next to the examination table. "We're all very excited."

Yes. Excited. That's me. I can barely keep from urinating into my catheter.

"You're a rather unique specimen," says Bob, prepping the needle. "The only one who has reacted to our tests in the way we'd hoped. Which is why you're very important to our research."

If I'm that important, you'd think they'd give me a room with a view and preferred member status. Maybe a shave and a haircut. Or some decent toilet paper.

A year ago at this time, I was in a custom ten-by-ten cage at the SPCA in Santa Cruz, doing satellite interviews with CNN and Howard Stern while reclining on my queen-sized sofa bed and drinking Beringer Private Reserve Cabernet Sauvignon. So it's easy to understand why my expectations might be a little out of the ordinary. But really, I don't think I'm being unreasonable in hoping for some Charmin or a package of baby wipes.

With my head held in place I have a pretty limited view of my surroundings, but I see the elevated viewing area at one end of the examination room, where a man with dark hair and a 1970s porn star mustache enters and sits down in the front row behind the Plexiglas window. Joining him is a tall, attractive woman with a bald head. I've seen both of them numerous times during my stay here, watching me from the viewing area or from behind splatter shields, talking to one another. I've never heard what they're saying, but I'm guessing they're not discussing my health plan.

While I'm watching the two of them, Bob sticks the needle in my shoulder. There's no pain or any sense of discomfort. I don't even feel the needle go into my flesh. It's really not much more than the sensation of having a fly land on my shoulder.

That's one of the advantages of being a zombie. You can stub your toe or get your arm torn out of its socket and you don't really notice much of a difference. Except when you stub your toe it doesn't impact your ability to tie your shoes or clap your hands.

Bob reaches over and pulls a flat-screen monitor into view above me. The monitor is attached to an arm, like the overhead light in a dentist's office, only I don't think this is covered by my dental insurance. Bob positions the monitor above me so that it's directly in my line of sight, then he inserts a speculum into each of my eyes, forcing my eyelids open.

He was right. This *is* new.

"Comfy?" asks Bob.

He walks around to the cart on the other side of me, where the electrodes attached to my head are connected to the machine with all the switches and needles and gauges. I still don't know what the contraption is, but from the looks of it, I'm guessing it doesn't measure happy thoughts.

Bob puts his particle mask back on and tightens the straps, then he adjusts his safety goggles. "Don't worry about these. They're just a precaution. Standard procedure."

That's easy for him to say. He's not the one strapped

to a cadaver tray in an examination room with his eyes clamped open and his head hooked up to some machine. I'd like to switch places with Bob and see if he still thinks it's just standard procedure.

While Bob fiddles with some of the knobs and levels, I glance at the mustached man and the bald woman, who are both leaning forward and watching with interest.

"Okay, it looks like we're all set." Bob turns and looks up at the viewing room and gives the thumbs-up. The mustached man nods his head once while the bald woman stares down at me, her eyes looking directly into mine. Under normal circumstances I'd say we were sharing a moment, but normal and I haven't spent a lot of time together lately.

"I hope you're a fan of the cinema," Bob says to me.

On the monitor above me, the blue screen is replaced with video clip, a scene from the original *Night of the Living Dead,* where the zombies are chowing down on barbecued Tom and Judy.

"Lights, camera, action," says Bob.

Then he turns on a switch and white light explodes behind my eyes.

TWO

Several hours of video clips of zombies eating humans later, I'm back in my cage, which isn't nearly as nice as my accommodations when I was at the SPCA in Santa Cruz, but I'm trying to make the best of a bad situation. True, this isn't exactly the Ritz-Carlton, but things could be worse. I could be in a zombie zoo. Or slowly decomposing while I'm staked down in a body farm. So all things considered, I should consider myself lucky.

At least I'm not in a cadaver drawer.

My cage is seven by seven by seven, which gives me forty-nine square feet and a little under 350 cubic feet of living space. Not enough room to do wind sprints, but I get to stretch my legs occasionally and get in a few push-ups and sit-ups. Zombies aren't known for their physical fitness and cardiovascular health, but I need to do something while I'm in here to keep from losing my mind. Though sometimes I wonder if it hasn't already been misplaced. Or taken from me.

When you've spent a year being tortured and confined to a cage while trying to forget about everything you've lost, keeping a positive outlook can become a bit of a challenge. Mostly I'm just going through the motions and trying to connect with my inner zombie Buddha.

I've tried meditating to maintain some mental balance, but when someone comes by every couple of hours to stab you or shoot you or hose you down with cold water, it's kind of difficult to find your spiritual center.

I look around at the other cages, twenty-four in all and most of them occupied with other zombies, an almost even split between males and females. During the time I've spent here, I've seen hundreds of zombies come and go, some of them staying in the kennel for a few months and others not sticking around for more than a day or two before they disappeared. None of my current neighbors has been here more than a couple of months.

I'm like the dean of the zombies.

While the majority of my prison mates are wearing green hospital gowns to maintain some semblance of self-respect, we do have a couple of exhibitionists in the group—Hillary, who lives three cages down and one row over, and Patrick, who lives right next door.

Patrick is standing up in his cage and staring at me, providing an unsolicited glimpse of full frontal nudity. While I find it a little odd that he's so comfortable being naked, I appreciate Patrick's company. Most of the other zombies who've been in and out of here tend to keep to themselves, but Patrick makes an effort to engage me in zombie charades and inquire as to my general well-being.

Right now, he's holding his right hand up with the

tips of his thumb and index finger connected in a circle with a questioning expression on his face. I give him the okay sign back, then I stand up and slip into my hospital gown because I'm not comfortable being naked.

That and I don't want to compete with the fact that Patrick is considerably more well-endowed than me. Not that I've noticed or anything.

Some of the other zombies give me a glance or a nod but most of them are insular communities of one. Since our mouths are all sewn shut, there's not a whole lot of conversation or communal sharing of experiences going on. And no one's screaming *It's a madhouse!* at the top of his lungs like Charlton Heston. We're just a quiet little group of nearly two dozen reanimated corpses minding our own business and existing in silence.

It's kind of like being at a Trappist monastery, only with stun batons.

However, even though there's not any talking, we have managed to communicate and learn one another's names through some basic hand gestures. Mostly we just sleep and sit around and stare at each other and excrete waste while we wait for one of the interns or lab techs to come and take us—sometimes for feedings, sometimes for tests, sometimes for something from which we never return.

Although my legs have grown somewhat weak from a lack of any significant physical exercise, I'm still in better shape than most of the others. While I have lost weight, I don't have any visible injuries or suppurating wounds or signs of decomposition. It didn't hurt that I'd been eating a steady diet of Breather before I arrived and that whatever they're feeding me is helping to keep my coat bright and shiny.

About half of my neighbors, however, suffer from a host of afflictions, including bloat and sloughage—which is when liquid from deteriorating cells gets between layers of skin and loosens them, often causing large sheets of skin to peel off. Sloughage is one of the largest causes of depression among zombies, along with tissue liquefaction and maggots. Being undead isn't easy. The name-calling and the lack of rights aside, you just never expect to have to deal with the day-to-day problems of being a reanimated corpse.

If you've never had to deal with a maggot infestation while your brain liquefies and bubbles out of your ears and mouth, then you probably wouldn't understand.

However, not all of my neighbors' physical problems are the result of nature taking its course. Nearly all of them have been shot, stabbed, blinded, poisoned, neutered, burned, sprayed with pesticides, subjected to chemical burns and toxicity tests, or had patches of skin and internal organs removed. A couple of former inmates had their bodies dismantled piece by piece until they were nothing more than an empty torso so the researchers could observe how long they would survive.

In addition to these experiments, a number of my brethren have been injected with crystal methamphetamine, given cancerous tumors, had drain cleaner dripped into their eyes, had their eyes sewn shut, their ears cut off, and holes drilled into their bones and skulls.

These are some of the same experiments they used to do on animals. Now they conduct these tests on us, instead. It makes you wonder how far Breathers will go in order to extend their lives, get better drugs, or develop cosmetics that don't cause allergic reactions.

I pace around my cage in an attempt to exercise my atrophied muscles as Patrick watches and scratches at himself absently. This isn't exactly the future I had planned for myself. And while it would be easy to lay the blame somewhere else—my parents, society, anticannibalism laws—ultimately, the only one I have to blame is me. My actions led me to this point, beginning a year and a half ago when I fell asleep behind the wheel of my car and slammed into a redwood tree, killing my wife and orphaning my seven-year-old daughter.

Rachel is buried in the Soquel Cemetery, seven hundred miles away. Although I've since done my grieving for her and moved on, I've had plenty of time to recount all the ways I could have been a better husband. Like spending less time reading the paper. Or paying more attention to her emotional needs. Or not falling asleep while driving home and killing her.

The last time I saw Annie, she was waving good-bye from the front porch as we drove off to that dinner party in San Francisco from which we never returned. After the accident, Annie went to live with Rachel's sister in Monterey. Due to the lack of visitation rights given to zombies, I wasn't allowed to see her. And as far as I know, her aunt and uncle and grandparents shielded Annie from the truth of my reanimation.

I think about Annie a lot—how she's doing and if she ever found out about her father, about what I became. I'm guessing it was kind of hard for her to remain ignorant of the fact that her father was a zombie after I appeared on a bunch of television and network news programs to promote zombie civil rights. But even if Annie didn't see those interviews, she probably heard the news about the attack on Sigma Chi and the ensuing confrontation on the Pacific Coast Highway.

I still remember all of the police and military vehicles that surrounded us. Dozens of Breathers with weapons and body armor against just two dozen zombies with nowhere to run or hide. We never stood a chance. But we didn't give up. We fought for what we believed in, for our right to exist, but in the end nothing changed. And instead of going out in style, I ended up getting Tasered and captured and knocked unconscious, only to wake up in this place.

I try not to think about that night. About what happened to Rita and to Jerry and to all of the other friends I lost. Except they were more than just friends. They were my family. Tom, Carl, Helen, Naomi, Zack, Luke. Even though they were all there with me that night, I don't know if anyone survived or escaped or ended up in another research facility like me, but one way or another, I lost them.

When I died in that car crash eighteen months ago I thought I'd lost everything—Rachel, Annie, the life I'd lived. But then I found a reason to go on, a purpose to exist, and a new family who loved and cared about me. I'd found something that mattered, something to look forward to, only to once again lose everything.

While I often reminisce about my friends and everything we went through together, it still hurts to think about them. Especially Rita. I see her face nearly every time I close my eyes—her crimson lips, her alabaster flesh, her disarming gaze—and my lifeless heart still pounds. But I can't allow myself to think about what happened to her. Not if I don't want to completely lose my mind.

So instead I try to think about my memories of Annie. Going to the beach and playing at the park and opening presents on Christmas morning. All of the smiles and the giggles and the wide-eyed wonder. I have seven years of good memories of Annie to keep me company while I'm in here. And that's about the only thing keeping me sane and giving me anything that resembles joy.

But sometimes, even the good memories can be painful when you realize the extent of everything you've lost.

I'm getting melancholy again.

After a few minutes I stop walking around my forty-nine square feet of opulence and I look around at the other zombies sitting in their cages, and I wonder what their lives were like before they died and reanimated and ended up in here. Where they lived. Who they loved. What they lost.

In the cage on one side of me sits Orrin, who is blind in one eye and showing signs of the initial stages of bloat, while in the row of cages behind me, Deirdre braids what's left of Melanie's hair through the bars between their cages and Buck picks at the empty cavity that used to be his nose as yellow fluid drips from several wounds in his chest. Most of the others are either pacing around in their cells, sleeping, or staring into the abyss of their inevitable insanity.

Or maybe I'm just projecting.

On the other side of me, Patrick knocks on the bars of his cage. When I turn to look at him, he's holding up six fingers.

"Hhht. Lll mmm mmm, nnt hhh?"

When your lips are sewn shut, you tend to speak mainly in consonants.

I have no idea what Patrick's trying to say, and I wish he'd put on his surgical gown because I'd rather not notice that he's got a half woodie, but I don't want to be rude, even if he is the one who's pointing. So I sit down and Patrick follows suit, which cuts down on the surface area of nakedness.

While Patrick's only been here a couple of weeks, I've communicated with him more than with any of the other dozens of zombies who have stayed in the cages next to mine, mostly because of Patrick. He has this happy-go-lucky way about him that's difficult to ignore. Kind of like a golden retriever who wants to play fetch. He's relentless. And I have to admit, most of my neighbors have been surly and bitter, so it's nice to have the company of someone who seems oblivious to his circumstances.

When your home is a kennel full of decomposing corpses, it's always nice to have a breath of fresh air.

Patrick gives me a closed-mouth smile, seems to consider what he wants to say, then holds up a single finger for the first word, followed by a single finger for one syllable, and we play another game of zombie charades.

THREE

Shannon sits in the video room, looking at the monitors on the feed from the kennel, watching RC-1854 communicate with the zombie in the neighboring cage. She knows she should probably go home and get some rest, but she doesn't feel like leaving just yet.

She runs a hand over her eyes and forehead, then across her shaved scalp, enjoying the feel of her smooth skin before massaging some of the kinks in the back of her neck. Then she takes a drink of her long-cold coffee and keeps watching.

"You like watching it, don't you?" says Carter.

Shannon turns to find Carter standing inside the doorway, watching the monitors, though she knows he was probably watching her, as well. She doesn't know how long he was standing there, but she wouldn't be surprised if he'd been there for an hour. Carter watches everything.

She turns back to the monitors. "It beats watching reality television."

Carter walks up and stands beside her, stroking his mustache with his thumb and index finger like he's trying to stretch it across his upper lip. He's always stroking his mustache. Shannon's not a fan of facial hair, but Carter seems to have a love affair with his.

"It's perfectly understandable," says Carter.

"What is?"

"Your interest in it," says Carter. "It's a rather fascinating specimen."

Carter never refers to any of the Reanimants as *he* or *she,* but always as *it.* While he doesn't discourage the rest of the handlers and researchers from using proper pronouns when discussing their undead subjects, he forbids the use of names.

It humanizes them, he reminds everyone. Lest anyone forget that zombies are not human.

Shannon nods. "Yes, he is fascinating."

"I hope I don't need to remind you about the danger of becoming emotionally attached."

"I'm not emotionally attached," says Shannon. "But I admire him for what he was able to do."

"You admire that it instigated a nationwide uprising of Reanimants?"

"I admire his ability to effect change," she says. "And the passion he inspired in others. That's not something you encounter on a daily basis, even in humans. And it's certainly not something you can just manufacture in a lab."

"Give us time," says Carter. "I'm sure we'll come up with something."

Shannon sits in silence for several moments as Carter remains standing, both of them watching the monitors.

"Just make sure you don't confuse that inspired passion with compassion," says Carter, staring straight ahead without looking at her. "Because as soon as you see them as human, as soon as there's a flicker of doubt, that's when you've lost your ability to remain objective."

Then he turns and walks away, leaving her alone in the video room.

Shannon takes another sip of coffee and continues to watch the kennel full of zombies, but mostly she watches Andy Warner—or "RC-1854," as she's supposed to think of him. She likes to come here and watch because she believes they can learn as much from observing him as they can from all the medical tests and experiments they've performed over the past twelve months. Carter doesn't agree. According to him, the only thing that matters is what happens in the lab and during the tests. Everything else is just wasted energy and mental masturbation.

While the general public knows about zombies being rounded up and shipped off to medical research facilities and body farms, they don't know what that research involves. They aren't aware that zombies are being used for more than just impact testing and forensic science. And that the testing has been going on for decades.

Why some of the dead reanimate is still unknown, although the most popular theory is that it's due to a dormant gene that reactivates upon death in a small percentage of the population. A genetic mutation similar to hypertrichosis, which switches on cells that cause hair to grow where it shouldn't. Only in the case of the living dead, the cells that are switching on cause more to grow than just hair.

For years, researchers have tried to duplicate the Resurrection Gene in normal cadavers, but without success. The best they managed to get was an occasional flexing of the hand or the opening of the eyes. Nothing that would lead to any significant breakthroughs in medical science or win anyone the Nobel Prize.

Then came the discovery that when zombies eat human flesh, the decomposition process reverses and their bodies begin to regenerate. Wounds heal. Bones knit. Senses return. But it doesn't stop there. Eventually the internal organs start functioning again. The kidneys filter waste. The lungs process air. The heart pumps blood.

In short, they come back to life. Only they're not truly alive. Once they stop receiving the benefits of human flesh, their bodies begin to deteriorate again. But if researchers could determine why and how this happens and re-create the process in the lab, if they could replicate the mutation that takes place in zombies, the applications to the living would be indispensable.

They could theoretically reverse the aging process. Cure cancer and AIDS. Make dying obsolete. In essence, they could bottle immortality.

That's Carter's vision, anyway. His dream. That's what they're working toward, and he doesn't want one of the other facilities in Texas or North Carolina or Tennessee to discover the fountain of youth before he does. From what Shannon knows about Carter, he isn't motivated by fame or fortune or accolades. Nobel Prizes and grants don't concern him. All he cares about is crossing the finish line first.

And in Andy Warner, it appears Carter has found his winning horse.

While the research team has managed to create a synthetic version of human flesh in liquid form that improves the general physical appearance of a majority of the reanimated corpses, it's typically not more than a temporary reversal lasting only a few weeks. Nearly half the time it doesn't work at all. The only Reanimant to show consistent positive results and maintain the appearance of a living, breathing human is Andy Warner.

They still have a number of experiments to run, but this is the closest they've been to unlocking the secrets of zombie DNA in more than a decade. With any luck, they can use Andy's unique physiology to come up with a cure for death. Perhaps even a cure for zombieism. There might even be some military applications.

According to Carter, there are no boundaries, only limited perceptions.

Whatever it is that makes Andy Warner special, Carter wants to use it for as many applications as possible. That way, he not only wins, but places and shows, as well.

While Shannon believes the work they're doing is necessary for the success of their research and the benefits it can provide to the human race, she sometimes wonders if it's moral and humane. She knows zombies aren't technically human, or even alive, but she can't help but wonder if her inability to sleep more than a few hours a night has anything to do with the burden of a guilty conscience. And she's never been comfortable with the idea of staking them down in the body farm and leaving them out to slowly decompose for the study of Reanimant Forensics. Though what those zombies are subjected to isn't much worse than what they're put through in the lab—getting stabbed and electrocuted, exposed to toxins and poisons and viruses, kept caged up in confined quarters like animals.

She can't even imagine what it must be like to live that kind of existence. Though Carter would be quick to point out that saying they're living is a misuse of terminology.

Shannon grabs her empty coffee cup and goes to refill it, thinking about Andy Warner and the other zombies and what it means to be human, then she returns and sits down and continues to watch him communicate with the other zombie. When he's done, Andy does his nightly push-ups and sit-ups and stretches before lying down on his side and closing his eyes. She watches him and wonders what he's feeling. What he's thinking. What he dreams about. If he has nightmares. If he understands how special he is.

She keeps watching him until he falls asleep.

FOUR

*L*ouis Armstrong's deep, gravelly voice emanates from the CD player as I lie on the queen-sized sofa bed in my cage at the SPCA with Rita curled up next to me. It's the night before Christmas last year. I'm dreaming and I don't want to wake up. As much as it hurts to remember, I like being here in this moment. If I could, I'd stay here forever, just the two of us listening to old-time jazz Christmas songs and eating candied Breather.

Armstrong's "Winter Wonderland" is followed by Judy Garland's rendition of "Have Yourself a Merry Little Christmas." I look over at Rita and ask if she wants to fool around. Rather than answering my question, she looks at me and says:

"Andy, do you miss your daughter?"

I WAKE TO the sound of a door closing and the other zombies stirring in their cages, mumbling and murmuring because that's the best they can do. For several moments I remain on the floor of my own cage with my eyes closed, trying to hold on to the sound of Rita's voice and the feel of her body pressed up against mine. But the memory slips away and all I'm left with is an emptiness inside, the cold, hard concrete beneath me, and her lingering question.

Andy, do you miss your daughter?

When Rita asked me about Annie last Christmas Eve, my answer was no. I didn't miss her. I couldn't afford to. She wasn't part of my existence anymore and missing her was just a waste of energy. At that point, I'd embraced my zombie nature and finally decided that my life as a Breather had closed behind me. I'd let go of Rachel and moved on with Rita and even though Annie was still alive, I'd done my grieving for her, as well, and moved on with my undeath.

Or that's what I told myself.

After a year with nothing to do but think about Rita and Rachel and all of those I cared about, I've come to realize that I miss my daughter more than I could have ever imagined.

With a sigh, I open my eyes and sit up, waiting to see if the intern or the lab tech is here to get me for another movie night.

For each of the past two days I've been hooked up to that machine with Bob standing at the controls, my eyes forced open and staring at the monitor. Each time it's the same thing. Zombie films and electric shock and Bob smiling and saying, "Lights, camera, action." And each time I've come back feeling like someone has set off a stick of dynamite inside my head.

I don't know how much longer this is going to go on, but I'm getting a little tired of watching zombie films. It's just the same thing over and over. Zombies eating humans. Humans talking about zombies. Mass hysteria. Whatever happened to originality?

I look over at the kennel entrance, where a man with short blond hair stands with his back to us as he glances out into the hallway through the small rectangular window in the door, like he's playing hide-and-seek. I'm thinking he just ducked in here to avoid someone or to take a break or to make himself feel better about his pointless life by tormenting some defenseless zombies. It happens. Some Breather with marital problems or who's having a bad day at work comes into the kennel and yells at us or threatens us with a stun baton or sprays us down with cold water for kicks.

But when the blond man turns around and walks over to the cages and starts unlocking each of them one by one, I realize he's not here to inflict his emotional baggage on us.

The other zombies all start getting to their feet and moving toward the back of their cages as the Breather moves from one cage to the next, unlocking each one. I've seen him around a few times but I can't remember his name until he reaches me and I see the name Kevin Knox on his OHSU identification badge.

"Wwwt rrr llll dnnng?" I say. Which, in research facility zombie speak, is *What are you doing?*

"I'm from PETZ," says Kevin, who apparently speaks

research facility zombie. "I'm getting all of you out of here."

PETZ is the People for the Ethical Treatment of Zombies, an American zombie rights organization that claims to be the only Breather zombie activist group in the world. Even before I was brought here I remember hearing stories about PETZ infiltrating research facilities and zombie zoos to free the undead from the unacceptable conditions of their existence. Their slogan: *Zombies are not ours to enslave, dismember, experiment on, or use for our entertainment.*

While sometimes their methods are radical or confrontational, you have to admire their philosophical stance. Especially if you're a zombie.

As soon as my door is unlocked, I step out of my cage. When the others realize Kevin's not there to torment them, most of them play follow-the-leader, including Deirdre, Melanie, and Buck, though several have remained in their cages, either too far gone to care or else they're suspicious of Kevin's motives. I can't blame them after what we've all been through. The fact that he's not carrying a stun baton is good enough for me. When Kevin unlocks Patrick's cage, Patrick walks out and gives him a bear hug, which I can tell makes Kevin uncomfortable on more than one level.

It's kind of odd standing here with nearly twenty other zombies, most of them damaged and decaying and me looking like the George Clooney of reanimated corpses. I feel a little guilty, as if I've somehow managed to get off easier than everyone else. A lucky stiff, so to speak. But then I remember how Bob put clamps on my testicles and pumped me full of electricity and it kind of evens things out.

Once all of the cages have been unlocked, Kevin goes back to the door and looks out the window into the hallway. Patrick, who apparently thinks this is a game of monkey see, monkey do, follows Kevin and looks over his shoulder.

"Okay," says Kevin, turning around to find Patrick standing right in front of him, naked and grinning, so Kevin steps to one side. "It's clear out in the hallway. The next shift doesn't come on for another half an hour, so you should encounter a minimum of staff members, plus there aren't any Handlers in the building, so you won't have to worry about them."

Handlers are the research facility staff members who specialize in handling the undead. In other words, they're the ones trained to make sure we don't misbehave, which usually involves the use of stun batons.

"However, as soon as one of you is spotted," says Kevin, "you probably won't have much time to get out of the building."

Which I presume means we're not getting the guided tour.

"Whht hbhtt rrr stchs?" asks Deirdre, pointing to her mouth.

"Your stitches?" says Kevin. "I'm sorry, but I don't have time to help you with your stitches. You'll have to find a way to remove them on your own."

That seems kind of shortsighted. How are we supposed to eat anyone in order to defend ourselves?

Hillary appears next to me, the zombie nudist yin to Patrick's yang, although her nudity is more of a lifestyle choice than a display of her feminine charms. One of Hillary's breasts has been removed, she has multiple stab and puncture wounds in her stomach and thighs, and a greenish fluid is bubbling out of her nose.

So she's not exactly *Playboy* centerfold material.

"Once you're outside, you're free to go wherever you want," says Kevin. "But the fastest way out of the building is to take the exit door at the far end of the hallway. There's a set of stairs that leads down to ground level. From there you can head north toward downtown, east toward the river, or west into the woods."

Apparently we're not getting limo service.

"Just make sure not to head for the fenced-in area," he says.

"Iii ntt?" asks someone.

"Because that's the body farm," says Kevin.

The only thing worse than what we're being put through in here is being staked down and left out to decompose on the side of a hill.

If you've never been fed on by maggots and crows and insects while you slowly liquefied into a pool of yellow mud, then you probably wouldn't understand.

"I'd suggest the woods until it gets dark. That will make it easier for you to find your way to shelter." Kevin glances out the window one last time, then he looks back at us. "Okay, the coast is clear. Everyone ready?"

We all nod or grunt or give our assent in one way or another. Orrin farts, but I'm guessing that's a reaction to the gases building up in his bloating stomach rather than an enthusiastic affirmation.

I glance back and notice that two of the cages aren't empty. In one of them a female zombie named Heather, the youngest and newest zombie, sits huddled and shaking in the corner, staring out at the rest of us with her eyes wide and her arms wrapped around her knees. In the other cage, Barry, the oldest one of us and missing his left leg below the knee, stands on his good right leg and gives me a wistful smile and a Macy's Thanksgiving Day Parade wave.

I wave back, wishing I could do something to help him. Then Kevin opens the door.

We all stream out of the kennel and into the hallway, which is bright and sterile and empty. To the left, less than twenty feet away, the hallway dead ends. To the right, what seems the length of a football field away, is a green neon EXIT sign above a single door that leads to the stairway Kevin mentioned. Between us and that exit door are a couple of adjoining hallways and a dozen other doors, some of them closed, some of them open. There aren't any clocks on the walls, so I don't know what time it is, but I'm guessing it's morning, when most of the research staff haven't yet made it into work.

We move down the hallway, some of us at a faster clip than others. Since I've been cooped up for the better part of a year, my legs aren't used to this much walking, so I find myself lagging behind. I listen for the sound of voices or shouting, any indication that we've been spotted, but the only thing I hear is the muted shuffle and slap of bare feet on the floor and the sound of Orrin farting.

At some point I look around and realize Kevin isn't with us. A voice inside my head tells me that this is all a setup. That Kevin isn't really working for PETZ but is just putting us through some kind of psychological experiment to see how we'll react. Kind of like setting a bunch of mice loose in a maze to find out how smart they are. But at this point, I figure I might as well see if I can find the cheese.

The closer we get to the exit door, the faster everyone starts walking, sensing freedom just out of reach, and it's all I can do to keep up. The others pass the last adjoining hallway without incident and it seems like we're going to make it without anyone catching us. But when I glance down the hallway as I walk past, I see a woman in a lab coat staring in my direction, her eyes open in a moment of what I can only presume to be disbelief. Then she points and opens her mouth in a way that reminds me of Donald Sutherland at the end of *Invasion of the Body Snatchers*.

"Hey!" she shouts.

Not as creepy as the alien scream that comes out of Sutherland's mouth, but it does the trick. Everyone starts running.

The thing about real zombies is that we don't stagger and lurch around like your classic horror film zombies, but instead can run fast like the new and improved

Hollywood version. Unless you've spent the past twelve months cooped up in a cage. Then you're barely nosing out Frankenstein's Monster and the Mummy in the hundred-yard dash.

Up ahead of me the other zombies are escaping into the stairwell, a steady flow of animated cadavers pouring through the open door. Behind me I hear the sound of feet running along the hallway. I look back, expecting to see Breathers with stun batons coming around the corner at any moment, when my legs betray me and I stumble to the floor.

So much for beating Frankenstein's Monster.

Three lab techs reach the junction of the hallways and come to a sliding stop. They're just staring and watching, no stun batons to be had, looking more like they're trying to figure out what to do and how to do it and if their medical insurance covers something like this. Then someone's grabbing hold of me and helping me to my feet. It's Patrick, and I've never been so happy to see his naked body. Together we run the last ten feet to the exit door, banging it open and heading down the stairs. Fortunately it's only two flights to the ground floor and by the time we get there, the others have made it outside. Above us, the stairway remains silent and empty of lab techs. Apparently chasing after an escaped horde of zombies isn't in their job description.

Once we get out we discover it's morning, I'm guessing not long after sunrise, as there's a solid gray cloud cover and a steady mist falling. Most of the others are standing on the asphalt, looking around, trying to figure out which way to go.

We're in a parking lot behind the research facility. At the southern end of the lot, opposite the buildings, is a tall wooden gate bordered on each side by a ten-foot-high fence topped with razor wire that surrounds a tree-covered hillside, which I'm guessing is the body farm. Beyond that and to the west are the woods, which is where Kevin suggested we hide. Personally, I'd rather find someplace dry and warm with indoor plumbing and maybe a personal masseuse, but considering we're all barefoot and two of us are naked while the rest are wearing nothing but turquoise hospital gowns and sporting festering wounds, we're likely to draw attention to ourselves in the harsh reality of sunlight. So Kevin probably knew what he was talking about.

I'm just turning to Patrick to point to the woods and I start moving that way when we hear the sound of approaching sirens.

Everyone scatters.

FIVE

Patrick and I are running through the woods. Rather, Patrick is running and I'm doing my best to keep up with him, but my legs aren't in a cooperating mood.

While I might be a better-looking physical specimen than most of the other zombies, when you're running through the woods to avoid being captured by Breathers, function trumps form every time.

The rain continues to fall in a steady mist that at some point turns into a dependable drizzle. Fortunately the canopy is keeping us reasonably protected, which doesn't really matter from the standpoint of personal comfort, but corpses tend to decompose faster when exposed to water, so it's just common sense to try to keep yourself dry. Helps to cut down on fungal growth, which is tough to get rid of even with a good quality mold and mildew cleaner.

While some of the other zombies ignored Kevin's advice and took off toward downtown Portland or east toward the river, the rest, including Buck, Deirdre, and

Melanie, ran off into the woods ahead of us. But since I'm moving slower than Internet dial-up service, the others are so far ahead that we can't see any sign of them.

Behind us, down the hill, I hear the sound of voices. I presume Patrick hears them, too, since we're both running and not stopping to admire the scenery. It's been a year since I've seen a tree or smelled fresh air or felt the earth under my feet and I'd like nothing more than to take a few moments to enjoy being outside, but my personal moment of Zen will have to wait until we're not being chased by a mob of Breathers carrying stun batons.

The voices sound far enough away that they're not a threat to catch up to us anytime soon, but I'm slowing Patrick down and I know he's staying with me out of some sort of chivalrous zombie code, which I appreciate. But for that same reason, I can't let him get caught because of me.

I'm thinking I should head off in another direction and let Patrick continue into the woods. Problem is, he'd likely follow along, so I decide instead that the next-best thing is for me to find a place to hide on my own. And sooner rather than later.

We continue into the woods, me struggling along behind Patrick's naked ass and wondering if he was a nudist when he was alive or if he decided he might as well become one once he was dead, when we run past a fallen tree with a hollow opening large enough to fit a grown zombie.

I stop running and let out a grunt. When Patrick turns to give me a questioning look, I point at the dead tree and then to me, then to my legs. He shakes his head and I give him my best *this isn't up for discussion* look, then I hurry as fast as I can over to the tree and squeeze myself inside. It's not as roomy as it first looked and the accommodations aren't as nice as the cage I've been staying in, but it'll do for now. Though I'm glad I'm wearing a hospital gown and I'm not naked like Patrick because the inside of a dead tree isn't as smooth and polished as you'd like it to be.

Patrick runs over and stands outside the tree, looking around with this frantic expression like he's trying to figure out how he's going to fit inside with me. It's sweet, in a nude-zombie-on-the-run kind of way.

When he finally runs off, I think he's gone and I can stop worrying about him and instead focus on how I'm going to look inconspicuous lying here inside a dead tree. Then Patrick comes back with some tree branches that he uses to conceal the opening. He runs off again and comes back with some foliage, like he's building a nest. When he's done, my hiding place is better than it was to begin with.

Patrick squats down and peers in at me through a gap in the branches, a question on his face and his right thumb and forefinger held up in a circle. I smile and give him the okay sign back, then motion for him to go. He takes off into the woods. I watch until he's out of sight, then I take several deep breaths, trying to become one with the dead tree while finding my undead center. But when you're a reanimated corpse, peace of mind is about as hard to find as imagination at a Hollywood studio.

When I first came back from the dead, I would write the occasional haiku to help me deal with my new existence, a kind of artistic therapy to take away some of the sting of being a zombie in a world ruled by the living. I kept at it for the first few months at the research facility, composing haikus in my head and mumbling them to myself. I even rewrote the lyrics to "If I Only Had a Brain" from *The Wizard of Oz* to help me deal with my cravings for human flesh.

> *I could gnaw away the hours*
> *Delightfully devour*
> *Digesting Johns and Janes*
> *And my mouth I'd be fillin'*
> *While my hands were busy killin'*
> *If I only had some brains*

Eventually I fell out of the habit and lost my creative spark. Now, lying here on the edge of freedom, waiting to see if I get caught and taken back to an existence of degrading and inhumane captivity, it seems like a good time to try to put a positive spin on my current circumstances.

> *zombie on the run*
> *in search of his dignity*
> *no more stun batons*

I just hope whoever is pursuing us doesn't have cadaver dogs.

It doesn't take long for them to reach me. A few minutes, tops. I can't see all of them from my limited perspective, but I can see legs in olive green pants and torsos in black jackets and hands carrying stun batons. It sounds like there are at least a dozen of them spread out around me, canvassing the woods, searching for us and calling out to one another. And, as luck would have it, they have a dog.

I can hear it outside the tree, sniffing the branches and foliage that Patrick laid out. I press myself back as far as I can, my heart pounding and my palms sweating even though I'm technically dead.

Sometimes I think I liked it better when I didn't have physiological reactions to tense situations. It made being undead much more Buddhist. Then the dog suddenly takes off barking after Patrick's trail and all of the Breathers follow suit and I exhale my relief.

I don't know why the dog didn't detect me. Maybe Patrick has a stronger zombie odor than I do. Or maybe the dog just has a bad sniffer. Or maybe whatever they've been feeding me that prevents me from decomposing and keeps my heart beating gives me that fresh Breather smell. Whatever the reason, I'm glad they didn't find me.

I hope the same can be said for Patrick.

SIX

"**A**nnie!"

It's eight thirty in the morning and nine-year-old Annie Walker is drinking a glass of apple juice and watching *Dora the Explorer* on Nickelodeon. During commercial breaks she flips the channel to KQED or PBS to watch *Sesame Street* or *Dinosaur Train.* She'd rather watch *Phineas and Ferb,* but they don't get Disney XD.

"Annie!"

It's Friday morning, four days before Christmas, and Annie's home watching TV on the couch while eating instant oatmeal and cinnamon toast that she made for herself. Her mother is late for work because she overslept again. Annie isn't surprised, since her mother didn't get home until after two in the morning.

"Annie!"

She's been living in this apartment with her mother for nearly three years, ever since Annie's father died of sudden cardiac arrest at the age of thirty-five.

With a sigh, Annie gets up from the couch and walks

down the hallway and finds her mother in her bedroom, halfway dressed, looking through her closet—a lit cigarette in her mouth and her hair in need of a brush.

"There you are," says her mother. "Have you seen my blue turtleneck, kiddo?"

Annie looks at her mother and wonders when she last saw her without a cigarette or a drink or the smell of one of the other on her breath.

"It's in the laundry," says Annie. "You wore it out to dinner two nights ago and spilled red wine on it. Remember?"

"Shit." Her mother takes a quick drag on her cigarette and blows the smoke out in a single, exasperated huff. "I should have done laundry. Now I'll have to figure out something else to wear."

Annie watches her mother go through the clothes that are strewn across her floor and bed, picking up a sweater or a turtleneck here and there and smelling it or checking for stains and wrinkles.

"Why don't you wear your red sweater?" says Annie. "It's festive. You know, like Christmas."

She says this with the hopes that her mother will get the hint. That she'll buy some decorations and Christmas lights to put up out front. That she'll bring home a Christmas tree. That she'll remember her promise about taking Annie to see Santa Claus at the shopping mall.

"Good idea," says her mother, reaching into her closet and talking around her cigarette. "Red's a better color on me than blue, anyway. Thanks, kiddo."

Annie stands there watching her mother slip her arms

into the sweater and button it up, keeping the cigarette between her lips, not getting the hint. She considers mentioning something to her mother about Christmas trees and decorations and Santa but whenever she does, her mother just says, *Sure thing, kiddo. We'll do it tomorrow.*

And then tomorrow never comes.

"Something on your mind?" Annie's mother takes a final drag on the cigarette and then deposits it with a *hiss* in a half-empty bottle of beer on the bedside table.

Annie shakes her head.

"Okay then," says her mother, putting on a pair of earrings that Annie helped pick out for her mother's last birthday. "How do I look?"

Annie studies her mother, who in spite of her disheveled appearance really does look beautiful as far as Annie thinks, especially when she doesn't have a cigarette in her mouth or a beer in her hand. And Annie was right. Her mother really does look good in red.

"Awesome," says Annie. "Red suits you."

Her father used to say that to Annie all the time, though it wasn't always red. Sometimes it was blue. Sometimes purple. Sometimes pink. Sometimes it wasn't a color at all but a television show or a song or a cereal.

Froot Loops suits you.

And every time he said it, no matter what it was, it made her giggle.

"Okay then," says her mother, grabbing her purse and a pair of high heels that she tosses into a plastic bag. She looks at her watch. "Shit, I've gotta run."

Annie follows her mother to the front door and

watches as she puts on her rain gear. Even though she knows what the answer will be, Annie decides to ask.

"Mom, can we go pick out a Christmas tree today?"

"Oh honey, I'm sorry, I can't," her mother says, slipping into her raincoat. "I'm meeting someone after work."

Her mother is always meeting someone after work.

"We'll go tomorrow." Her mother squats down in front of Annie. "We'll get the best tree in the lot. I promise."

"Cross your heart and hope to die?"

"Oh, now why would anyone want to hope for that?" Her mother ruffles Annie's hair and gives her a reassuring smile that Annie answers with a halfhearted one.

"What time are you going to be home?" asks Annie.

"I don't know, kiddo," she says, putting on her raincoat. "But I don't want you to wait up for me, okay?"

"Okay."

"There are frozen dinners in the freezer and fresh milk in the refrigerator," says her mother, slipping into a pair of knee-high rain boots. "Don't forget to brush your teeth before you go to bed. And even though it's raining, promise me you won't watch TV all day."

"I promise."

"Good girl." Her mother kisses Annie on the top of her head. "And thanks for the help with my sweater, kiddo."

Then her mother walks out the door and closes it behind her.

Annie walks over to the window and looks out through the blinds, which are thin and faded and cheap, with several broken slats and a pulley that no longer works, so as a result, the blinds are always down. She watches as her mother walks to her car, a red Honda Civic, and climbs inside. A few moments later she's pulling away from the curb and driving off down the street into the rain.

Once her mother's car disappears from view, Annie looks at the houses across the street from the two-bedroom apartment. The homes look inviting to her, with their curtains and their yards and their porches. But mostly what she likes about them are their lights and their decorations and their Christmas trees on display through the windows.

While Annie enjoys looking at the homes, she wishes she and her mother lived in one of them and had a tree and lights and giant candy canes in their front yard. She remembers how their old apartment used to be decorated for Christmas and how her father used to sing Christmas songs and how he would sit with her and watch *Frosty the Snowman* and *Rudolph the Red-Nosed Reindeer* and then read her a story about Santa and his elves before she went to sleep.

Annie misses her father a lot, but she misses him even more at Christmas.

She wishes she would have asked her mother to come home early instead of going out so that they could go and buy Christmas decorations and pick out a tree.

She imagines the two of them putting up the Christmas lights together and decorating the Christmas tree and listening to Christmas songs.

But even if her mother promised they would do those things, chances are she would end up disappointing Annie again, so Annie would rather wish for something that was more likely to happen.

She continues to stare out the window at the homes across the street, at the trees in the forest spread out behind them for as far as she can see, watching the steady rain as *Dora the Explorer* plays on the television behind her, thinking about her father and Santa Claus, wishing it would snow.

SEVEN

I don't know how long I stay hiding in the dead tree. Maybe an hour, maybe two. Maybe less, maybe more. Time has a way of becoming irrelevant when you spend a year not having to worry about schedules and appointments and how long it takes you to heal from being shot and stabbed and sprayed with pesticides. But at some point I notice that it's started to snow.

The last time I saw snow was nearly four years ago when Rachel and I drove up to Tahoe for Valentine's Day and we took Annie with us. She was five years old at the time and had never seen snow before. I remember how excited she was when she first saw it and then screamed when we tried to get her to walk in it and then laughed with delight when Rachel lay down and made a snow angel. I remember how we sat in front of the window of the cabin we'd rented and she watched in silent fascination as the snow fell from the sky.

I can almost see her breath fogging up the window.

The sound of approaching voices shakes me from my

reverie. At first I can't tell which direction they're coming from or how many of them there are but it's apparent that they're happy, so I'm guessing the hunting party is returning victorious.

A few minutes later the zombie hunters walk past, laughing and making jokes and sharing war stories.

"Did you see how that one twitched when I shocked it?"

"That was the most fun I've had since playing zombie paintball."

Behind the first group of hunters, chained together and walking in single file, are half a dozen of my undead brethren, including Deirdre, Buck, and Melanie. They all look despondent and hopeless and stare at the ground in front of them as they trudge back to their imprisonment. I'm hoping Patrick isn't one of those who got captured, that he managed to get away, but then I see him, bringing up the rear like a naked zombie caboose.

He doesn't give more than a moment's glance my way when he passes, but it's enough for me to see the fear and disappointment on his face. Then he's gone from view, followed by another handful of hunters, their stun batons unholstered and ready for action.

I watch them until they're out of sight but I can still hear them, their voices fading as they continue down the hill back toward the research facility. They're almost out of range when there's suddenly a commotion right outside of the tree. Something is moving around in the dead leaves and brushing up against the cover of branches and foliage. I think it's one of the dogs come back to find me but then I hear a loud squawking and trilling. It takes me a moment to realize there's a bird outside trying to get into the tree. And it sounds pissed off.

There's a flutter of wings and I hear the bird hopping around on the dead trunk, continuing to squawk and occasionally pecking at the wood, making a lot of noise. I'm afraid it's going to draw the attention of the hunters but they're apparently too caught up in their revelry to notice or investigate.

Rather than waiting around for the bird to give up and go away, I listen to make sure I can't hear the voices anymore, then I push the branches aside and crawl out from my hiding place. A woodpecker struts back and forth on the tree, voicing its displeasure, then it reprimands me one last time before reclaiming its home.

I look around, trying to decide which way to go. While continuing into the woods is probably the safest bet, I don't know if all of the hunters returned or if there are others still out there looking for zombies. And heading back toward the research facility is about as smart as playing Russian roulette with a cannon. So I head north through the trees, looking behind me every ten paces, expecting to see hunters coming after me, until I come upon a hiking path that takes me past a picnic area and across a wooden footbridge. Eventually I emerge from the woods in a cul-de-sac next to a lichen-covered sign that says NO PARKING AT ANY TIME and another sign that says DEAD END.

At least the symbolism has a sense of humor.

The street is only half a block long, with three houses

on one side and a tangle of trees and vines and brush across from them. At the other end of the block, just past the trees, the street curves to the right and disappears from view.

From the looks of it, no one's home at any of the three houses—two of which are plain and unadorned, while the third, the one in the middle with a white picket fence, has lights running around the windows and elves in the front yard with half a dozen reindeer hitched up to a sleigh. There are also giant candy canes and wrapped packages. A sign near the white picket fence says SANTA'S WORKSHOP and another sign says NORTH POLE.

The snow is still falling and no one's around, but it's not dark enough for me to take a stroll through the neighborhood looking like an escaped mental patient. Someone's bound to notice me, so I make my way across the street and head around the side of the first house and through a gate into the backyard, looking for a way inside so I can grab something to wear that's a little less *One Flew Over the Cuckoo's Nest,* but the house is locked up tight.

As I'm trying one of the windows to see if it will open, I see my reflection in the glass and I stop and stare. While I've caught faint, fleeting glimpses of myself in safety goggles and metal surfaces and the occasional Plexiglas splatter shield, I haven't had a good look at my face in nearly a year.

I reach up to touch my long white hair and my thick, white beard. I don't know what caused them to turn white. Maybe all of the stress I've been through. Or a side effect of what they've been feeding me. Whatever the reason, I don't look like me. Not my mental image of me, anyway. The face looking back is a complete stranger.

I stare at my reflection a few moments longer, then I turn to leave and find a pair of small pruning shears next to some gloves on the back porch. Using one of the windows to see what I'm doing, I cut the threads sewn across my lips. It only takes a couple of snips to do the job. It takes a little longer to pull out all of the threads, but in a couple of minutes the stitches are gone and I'm able to open my mouth for the first time in a year. It's strange, kind of like discovering that you have an orifice you'd forgotten existed. Then I use the pruning shears to cut off the feeding tube sticking out of my abdomen.

There's no way for me to get into the backyard of the second house and my legs won't cooperate when I try to climb over the fence, so I sneak back around to the front of the first house, looking for a way in, without any luck. The middle house doesn't have a side gate or access to the backyard, so I step over the white picket fence surrounding the North Pole and make my way to the front porch, ducking behind elves and reindeer as I go.

When I reach the porch, I notice a full-sized and fully clothed Santa Claus sitting in the chair next to his sack of toys to the left of the front door. I didn't see him when I first came out of the woods, but he looks about the right size for a nearly naked zombie.

After double-checking to make sure no one's watching, I walk up the steps, pull Santa down out of sight behind the shrubs and porch railing, and start undressing him. Turns out he's just a mannequin with some pillows and foam stuffing and a wig and fake beard held on by an elastic band.

A few minutes later, I'm wearing Santa's suit, complete with gloves and boots that thankfully fit, though Santa's apparently a fifty-two regular and I'm a forty-four long. The pants are a little big and the belt won't hold them in place, so I grab one of the pillows and stuff it into my pants, then cover up the rest with the jacket, giving me that bowl-full-of-jelly look. I come complete with my own white beard and hair, so the wig and fake beard go into the bag of toys. Once the hat is in place, I'm good to go.

Ho ho ho.

I walk down the porch and start across the front lawn to the gate, planning to head off down the street to see if I can find someplace safe to hide or some other zombies to give me shelter, when I hear the sound of a car approaching, coming up the hill. I freeze, not sure what I should do, then I turn around and head back to the porch, where I shove the mannequin into the bushes and my hospital gown into Santa's sack of toys, then sit down in the chair and do my best to look like I'm not alive. Which I'm hoping shouldn't be a problem.

That's when I notice that my Santa hat fell off and is lying in the middle of the front yard.

EIGHT

When it finally starts to snow, Annie doesn't waste any time putting on her galoshes and her parka and going outside. She knows there won't be enough snow to build a snowman or make snow angels, but it's been raining nearly the entire first week of Christmas break and she wants to see all of the Christmas decorations her neighbors put up.

Plus when she wished for it to snow Annie didn't believe it would actually happen, so when it does, she wonders if she can make some more wishes come true.

Like wishing for a Christmas tree. And for her mother to come home early. And for a stuffed panda bear.

So she wanders around her neighborhood, stopping in front of homes with lights and wreaths and nativity scenes, making her wishes at every stop. While Annie likes the little baby Jesus and all of the barnyard animals, she prefers the decorations with reindeer and elves and plastic Santas in the front yard. She figures if anyone could help make her wishes come true it's Santa Claus.

If only she could meet the real Santa, then maybe everything would be okay.

After exploring most of her neighborhood, Annie starts to walk up the hill at the end of her street. There are only three houses on the block at the top of the hill, but the house in the middle is the best one in the neighborhood, because they always put up decorations for Halloween and for the Fourth of July and even for Valentine's Day. But Annie's favorite is when Christmas comes around and the front yard is transformed into a winter wonderland.

A police car drives past her and continues up the hill, then makes a U-turn in the cul-de-sac and comes back down, the officer behind the wheel giving Annie a wave and a smile, which she reciprocates.

When Annie reaches the top of the hill, a smile spreads across her face at the sight of the elves and reindeer and sleigh in the front yard of the middle house, with a sign that says NORTH POLE. Christmas lights outline the front of the house, hanging from the roof like icicles. Giant candy canes are everywhere. And up on the porch, sitting in a chair by the front door next to his bag of toys, is Santa Claus himself.

Annie knows it's not the real Santa, just like she knows that the ones at the shopping malls and who stand outside downtown on the streets ringing their bells aren't real, either. There's only one Santa and he lives at the North Pole and he doesn't have time to hang out in malls or volunteer for the Salvation Army. He's got a list of more than a billion children to deal with, some of them who've been naughty and some of them who've been nice. And as far as Annie knows, Santa doesn't own a cloning device, so he has to take care of everything himself.

The fact that Annie hasn't received what she's wanted for Christmas the past three years hasn't compromised her faith in Santa. She figures he deserves some slack with all of the children in the world asking him for toys and computers and video games. But she hopes this year he comes to see her and brings her what she wants most of all.

Annie walks up to the front of the house and stands at the gate, near a sign proclaiming that this is indeed Santa's Workshop. Elves are hard at work surrounded by gift-wrapped presents and candy canes while the reindeer wait patiently for the sleigh to be filled with toys. With the snow falling and collecting on the ground, Annie could almost believe this *is* the North Pole.

She looks up at Santa sitting on the front porch and imagines that he sees her standing there. He calls out for her to come and sit on his lap, then invites her in for some cookies and hot chocolate and to meet Mrs. Claus. She's caught up in the fantasy, pretending she can smell the freshly baked cookies, when she notices Santa's hat on the ground in the front yard.

Annie opens the gate and walks up the path, between two elves who are both carrying brightly wrapped packages, and picks up Santa's hat before walking up to the porch. She rings the front doorbell and waits. When no one answers, she turns to the Santa sitting in the chair, his eyes open and staring straight ahead.

In the shadows of the porch, she thinks he looks almost real.

Annie thinks it's the best-looking fake Santa she's ever seen. Even his hair and beard look real, not like those beards most of the other Santas wear, which makes it obvious they're just pretending to be Santa.

She's heard some of the kids at school talking about how their parents pretend to be Santa, dressing up and filling their stockings and wrapping their presents. They claim their parents are really the ones who eat the milk and drink the cookies and that Santa Claus is just a fairy tale made up by adults to trick kids into being good.

A lot of the kids in her class have stopped believing in Santa Claus, which makes it harder for Annie to keep believing, but she wants to believe in Santa. She wants him to be real. She *needs* him to be real.

She reaches up to put the hat on his head and imagines the stuffed Santa coming to life, just like in *Frosty the Snowman* when they put the top hat on him, but she knows that things like that only happen in cartoons and movies.

When she's done, she steps back and admires her work before she decides the hat's a little crooked. When she leans in to fix it, Santa blinks and Annie lets out a little gasp.

She takes a step back and stares at him, waiting for

him to blink again. When he doesn't, she takes a step closer and whispers, "Is it you?"

He doesn't say anything at first, but now she can see that he's looking right at her.

"It's really you, isn't it?" she whispers as she takes another step forward and leans in closer. "You're Santa. The *real* Santa."

He keeps looking at her, like he's thinking about his answer, then he blinks again and gives her a single nod and a small smile. His mouth is covered by his bushy white beard, but Annie can see the smile in his eyes.

"I knew it, I knew it!" she says, hugging him. "I knew it was you!"

Santa's arms go around her and he holds her tight and it's all she can do to keep from bursting out in delighted giggles, though she notices that Santa smells like he could use a bath. Then he lets go and she stands up and looks at him with a big grin on her face.

"Do you know who I am?" she asks.

He doesn't answer right away but just stares at her, his eyes blinking. Annie's smile starts to falter as she's afraid he doesn't know who she is.

Then he says her name.

NINE

"**A**nnie?" I say.

It's the first word I've spoken in more than a year and it comes out barely more than a whisper. I know this little girl standing in front of me can't possibly be my daughter, my Annie, but for a few moments I can swear it's her.

Then I realize it's just a little girl who looks about the same age as Annie. Not to mention she has the same color hair and eyes.

And as luck would have it, it turns out they have the same name.

"I knew you remembered me!" she says, hugging me again.

It's been a year since I've had physical contact with another human being that didn't involve being poked or prodded or shoved into a cage, and it feels so good I don't want to it to end. But it occurs to me that I might not exactly smell like candy canes and pine needles, so I let her go and she steps back and stares at me, a big smile on her face that I can't help but return.

When her smile fades and a look of concern replaces it, I wonder if she's on to me.

"What are you doing in Portland, Santa?" she asks. "Aren't you supposed to be at the North Pole?"

"I was at the North Pole," I say, my voice coming out dry and dusty as I attempt to lower it an octave like your average shopping mall Santa. "But the next thing I knew, I was here."

I hope she doesn't ask too many difficult questions because I'm a little unprepared to play Santa. I was just looking for something to wear, not become a holiday icon.

Annie stares at me, her eyes going wide. "Did I bring you here?"

"Yes," I say, standing up. "And I should probably be getting back."

I have no idea where I'm going, but I need to get off this porch before the owners come home or another police car decides to make a drive-by. Or half a dozen men emerge from the woods carrying stun batons.

Annie follows along after me as I make my way down from the porch and across the front lawn. "Are you okay, Santa? You're walking kind of funny."

"One of the reindeer kicked me."

"Which one?"

"Rudolph."

"That wasn't very nice."

"No," I say. "It wasn't. He still has a lot of issues."

I'm trying to figure out what to do and where to go when I realize that at some point I'm going to have to go back to the research facility to rescue Patrick and the others. At least Patrick. I owe him that much for helping me escape. But I know I can't do it alone, which means I'm going to need to find some help. Some local zombies or maybe some members of PETZ.

But first, I need to find someplace to hide until it gets dark.

"Do you want to come over to my place for some milk and cookies, Santa?" says Annie. "Before you go back to the North Pole?"

Well, that was easy.

I look down at Annie, at her innocent face looking up at me, wearing a hopeful smile. The idea of hiding at Annie's sounds tempting, though I'm pretty sure Annie's parents won't be too happy about their daughter bringing home a stray Santa.

Adults tend to be a little less accepting than small children when it comes to zombies and strangers in Santa suits.

"Are your parents home?"

"Mom won't be home until late," says Annie. "Probably not until after midnight."

"What about your father?"

Annie looks down at the ground, her hands shoved into her coat pockets. "My dad died three years ago."

I stand there trying to come up with something to say, something Santa-ish to make her feel better, but I'm guessing now isn't a good time for a hearty *Ho ho ho.*

"Maybe you could come over and keep me company until you have to go?" says Annie, looking back up at me. "I can even make hot chocolate, unless you prefer warm milk. But now that I think about it, I don't know if we have any cookies. How do you feel about Gummi Bears?"

While I'm not a big fan of Gummi Bears, my options for shelter are pretty limited and I need to get off the street. Plus how can I say no to her? "Okay. But just for a little while."

"Yay!" Annie reaches out and takes me by the hand. "This is going to be so much fun!"

I get a flash of my daughter holding my hand and I'm momentarily overwhelmed with emotion. I can see us walking along the beach in Santa Cruz, the breeze blowing in off the ocean and the waves crashing and Annie asking me what makes the waves and how fish swim without any arms and legs and where all the water comes from. I can almost smell her shampoo and hear her voice and imagine that the past eighteen months never happened. Then my daughter and the beach are gone and Annie's leading me down the hill toward her apartment.

TEN

I'm sitting on the couch with Annie, in the middle of watching *The Year Without a Santa Claus* and drinking hot chocolate. It's just the instant stuff out of individual packets, but I haven't tasted anything since last New Year's Eve and it's like crack. I've had four cups already and I want more. Turns out there was a bag of Famous Amos chocolate chip cookies, so we polished off that, too.

I'm guessing my blood sugar levels are probably off the chart, but at this point I'm not real concerned about maintaining a balanced diet.

Outside the apartment, a light snow is still falling but the late afternoon hasn't quite yet given way to evening.

"Can I get you some more hot chocolate, Santa?" asks Annie.

"With marshmallows, please," I say, handing her my empty mug.

Annie puts the DVD on PAUSE, then goes into the kitchen to microwave another cup of hot chocolate while I get up to go to the bathroom, which is a luxury when you're used to relieving yourself into a pan or a cathe-ter or a drain in your cage. I also take the opportunity to shove another cotton ball into my chopped-off feeding tube because it's dripping.

I've already washed my hair and face and slapped on some Dove Clear Cool Essentials deodorant. Using soap and shampoo was like an orgasm for my face and head. Plus it gave my hair and beard that soft, luxurious feel and made me look even more like St. Nick.

Although I've used the bathroom several times already, I can't help staring at my reflection in the mirror. I still don't recognize myself, but then I'm not the Andy that I used to be. Not exactly new and improved. It's not as if I've spent the past twelve months in a chrysalis and have undergone some sort of metamorphosis into a zom-bie butterfly. But when you haven't seen your face in a year and it's not the one you remember, it takes a while to get reacquainted.

When I return from the bathroom, I smell the hot chocolate heating up and I find myself licking my lips in anticipation of another cocoa sugar rush. You'd think after a year of not being able to eat Breather that I'd be more interested in the savory delights of human flesh than Carnation Hot Chocolate. But while I am alone in an apartment with a nine-year-old girl who represents a good six square meals, I'm not a monster. After all, there are guidelines and common zombie etiquette when it comes to eating Breather.

I will not eat children.

I will not eat pregnant women.

I will not eat Special Olympics athletes.

I will not eat celebrities.

I will not eat career politicians.

This last one is really more of a guideline than a rule, but in general it's a good idea to avoid eating Breathers who might generate headlines or lead to police investigations. Maintaining self-control and using restraint is what keeps us from getting into trouble. Of course, I did eat my parents, my therapist, and killed a bunch of fraternity members in a fit of passionate vengeance, so maybe I'm not exactly the best one to be handing out advice.

However, sometimes you just can't help yourself when some douche bag in a movie theater pulls out his smartphone and starts texting.

Annie returns with my mug, then snuggles up next to me and resumes the video as Heat Miser and Snow Miser argue on the TV screen. I know I should be worried about Annie's mom coming home early and ruining the party, not to mention I just escaped from a zombie research facility that I'm planning to break back into without any idea of how I'm going to do it.

Just add it to my list of Things to Do.

But sitting here on the couch with Annie curled up next to me as we drink hot chocolate and watch Christmas specials reminds me of the life I once lived and the daughter I once had and it makes me feel almost happy.

Almost.

I don't want it to end.

Plus it's not yet dark outside, so I don't feel comfortable going out in public. While my disguise might fool a nine-year-old girl, I don't know how effective it's going to be on adults. So instead I sit and continue watching *The Year Without a Santa Claus* with Annie and let myself pretend that this is my reality.

"Santa, did you ever take a year off from Christmas?"

I look down at Annie, who is staring up at me with an innocent expression that only small children can nail. "You mean like what we're watching?"

She nods. "Did you ever feel like no one really cared about Christmas and stopped believing in you?"

Well, after I came back from the dead my parents stopped believing in me. So did all of my friends. Not to mention most of society. But I don't think I need to unload that particular baggage on Annie.

"No," I say. "I never felt that no one cared about Christmas. But sometimes adults stop believing in me."

"How come?"

"It's just what happens to a lot of people when they get older," I say. "They stop believing in all sorts of things."

"Like what?"

"Like Santa Claus. And magic. And heroes."

"That doesn't sound like much fun," she says.

"No, it's not."

We continue watching TV in silence. So far we've gone through *How the Grinch Stole Christmas, Frosty the Snowman, Mickey's Christmas Carol,* and *Rudolph the Red-Nosed Reindeer.* Annie says that while she likes Rudolph, even if he did kick me, she likes this Christmas special better because it's all about me.

"Then you've never taken a year off?" she asks, not looking up at me.

"Never."

There's something in the way she asks her question that sends off little alarm bells in my head. Like when your wife or your girlfriend says, *No, there's nothing wrong. I'm fine.*

"So if you've never taken a year off," she says, "then where have you been for the past three years?"

I look down at her and realize I'm in trouble.

"What do you mean, Annie?"

When she sits up and looks at me, I see tears welling up in her eyes. "How come you haven't come to visit me?"

I look around the apartment, which is clearly lacking in Christmas cheer. No tree. No lights. No stockings hung by the chimney with care. Although to be fair there's no chimney to begin with, just a wall heater, but I'm the only Christmas decoration in the place.

If Annie's mother were here, I'd give her a piece of my mind. Not literally, of course, but when you're a zombie that's always an option.

"I'm sorry, Annie," I say, feeling guilty, even though I didn't do anything wrong. Apparently this is something women learn to do to men at an early age. "Please don't cry."

Instead of helping, the tears come full force, spilling out of Annie's eyes and down her cheeks. It's like someone at the tear factory turned on a faucet.

"Haven't I been good?" she asks.

"Yes, Annie," I say, scrambling to come up with some way to comfort her. "You've been a very good girl. It's not your fault at all."

"Then what happened?" she says, the words coming out between sobs. "Why didn't you come to visit? How come you didn't bring me what I wished for?"

She sits there on the couch, her eyes red and her cheeks wet with tears, waiting for an answer. This playing Santa Claus is a lot more complicated than I'd imagined.

"Annie, you know how there are more people in the world now than there used to be?" I say.

She nods. "You mean like population growth?"

"Yes. Exactly. Well, for the past twenty years or so, because there are so many more children in the world, I've had to . . . hire helpers to deliver all of my presents."

She sniffles and rubs one of her eyes. "You mean like all of the fake Santas at the shopping malls?"

"Yes," I say. "The very ones. And because I have to work year-round making my list and checking it twice and matching up all of the good little girls and boys with their wish lists, I don't always have the time to double-check to make sure all of the toys get delivered."

I watch her, hoping she buys my answer because the rest of my Santa's bag of excuses is empty.

Annie wipes away some of her tears. "So you didn't forget about me?"

"Of course I didn't forget about you. I'm sorry you didn't get what you wished for, but it won't happen again."

"Promise?" she says.

Maybe it's because of the look in her eyes or the tears on her face or the way she reminds me of my daughter, but I make a vow I can't possibly keep.

"I promise," I say.

Whatever they injected me with at the research facility has apparently robbed me of the ability to make rational decisions. Either that or this Santa suit is going to my head.

"Cross your heart?" she says, her face brightening, a little ray of Annie sunshine peeking out from behind the clouds.

"Cross my heart," I say, performing the action to demonstrate my sincerity.

Annie's face breaks out in a smile, the sun coming out full and bright, and she leans in and gives me a big hug.

"And hope to die?" she says.

"Yes, Annie," I say, hugging her back. "And hope to die."

That's one part of the promise I know I won't have a problem keeping.

ELEVEN

Shannon walks through the woods just before sunset, her flashlight beam finding nothing but trees and snow and the five and a half feet of perpetual chatter that is her partner Duncan walking along ahead of her.

"I'm freezing my ass off," says Duncan, a flashlight in one hand and a stun baton in the other. "Aren't you freezing your ass off?"

Shannon wears a light jacket, her bald head unprotected from the falling snow, but she barely gives it a second thought. "I'm fine."

"Why aren't you cold?" he says. "I thought women were always supposed to be cold."

"Where did you hear that?"

"I didn't hear it," says Duncan. "It's a fact. Their feet are always cold. Their hands are always cold. They're always fucking cold."

"Well," she says, her flashlight beam disappearing into the woods, "I guess I'm not like most women."

"Yeah," says Duncan. "I've noticed."

They continue through the woods, their flashlights sweeping through the growing shadows and the falling snow. From what Recovery told them, a large group of the escaped Reanimants went this way. Most of them were rounded up not long after their escape. Animal Control picked up three more between OHSU and downtown, along with two others found hiding in a Dumpster out behind the Old Spaghetti Factory near the Willamette River.

That made fourteen recovered in all, which meant there were three escaped Reanimants still missing, one of them being Andy Warner.

So even though there were already two agencies and several dozen trained officials out looking for the remaining escapees, Carter sent Shannon and Duncan and half a dozen other Handlers out to find Andy. While Carter doesn't care about the other two zombies, he doesn't want anything to happen to his prized experiment and he doesn't trust the goons on Recovery or the incompetent burnouts who work for Animal Control.

Carter's words, not hers.

But after searching the woods most of the afternoon, all Shannon and Duncan ended up finding was a lot of trees and mud and snow.

"This is pointless," says Duncan. "We've been out here for more than four hours looking for him and we haven't found squat. Speaking of which, I have to take a dump."

"Thanks for sharing."

"Hey, it's just a normal biological function. You do it. I do it. Your parents do it. Even the queen of fucking England does it."

"That doesn't mean we have to discuss it."

"Fine by me," he says. "But I need to find a bathroom soon or else I'm going to end up dropping trou like a fucking bear."

She doesn't bother to tell him that bears don't wear pants.

"You ever drop trou in front of someone?" asks Duncan.

"I thought we were done discussing this."

"It's just a simple yes-or-no question."

"Is there a point you're trying to make?"

"Not really. Just making conversation. There doesn't always have to be a point to something."

"I know. It's one of your talents."

"What is?"

"Not making a point."

"I'll take that as a compliment."

They continue through the woods on their way back to OHSU, flashlight beams picking out trees and falling snow and the occasional woodpecker, but no zombies. When they come to a path that heads off in the direction of downtown, Shannon decides to take it.

"Where are you going?" says Duncan.

"This way," she says.

"Why?" asks Duncan, pointing down the hill. "Home base is that way."

"Because we're not done looking," says Shannon, then she walks away as Duncan follows along behind her, grumbling about the cold and the snow.

While she's more comfortable working alone, Shannon agreed to work with Duncan at Carter's request because none of the other Handlers, all of them men, could stand his constant chatter. Being the only woman Handler at the research facility in a male-dominated field has its challenges, most of which come from dealing with her human coworkers rather than from her undead test subjects.

She's worked with Duncan for two months now and even though he lacks an internal editor and runs on the chatty side, she prefers his company to the uptight and macho Handlers she's been paired with before.

"You still haven't answered my question," says Duncan from behind her.

"What question?"

"About going to the bathroom in front of someone else."

"Why do you want to know?"

"Just curious," he says. "Plus I'm trying to take my mind off the fact that I'm starting to crown."

Ten minutes later they emerge from the woods in a cul-de-sac next to a no-parking sign with three homes on one side of the street. The house in the middle is decked out and lit up with Christmas lights and decorations while the other two homes sit unadorned and wanting.

"So why are we here?" asks Duncan as they walk up to the first house.

"Because this is where he would find food, shelter, and clothing," she says. "They're the basic needs for survival that most humans have."

"Yeah, but it's not human."

Shannon knocks on the front door. If anyone answers, she'll make up a story about a lost cat and ask if the owners would mind if she looked for it out behind their house, but no one seems to be home.

"And how come you said *he*?" asks Duncan as they walk around the side of the house toward the back. "Don't you mean *it*?"

Duncan has adopted Carter's use of the gender-neutral reference. Whether it's because he agrees with Carter or because he's just playing the game, Shannon doesn't know. And she doesn't care.

"He used to be a human," she says, "so I'm giving him the courtesy of assigning gender."

"What does Carter think about your gender courtesy?" Duncan asks as they go through the gate into the backyard.

"I don't always worry about what Carter thinks," she says. "Now look for any signs he might have been here."

They sweep their flashlights across the ground as the last remnants of light disappear behind the clouds. While Duncan searches the yard, Shannon focuses on the back porch and the rear door and windows to see if someone might have tried to gain access to the house, but everything's locked. She's about to give up on finding anything when she notices a pair of gloves and pruning shears on the porch near the top of the steps. As she pans the light across the porch she finds several pieces of thick black thread and a three-inch-long piece of tubing nearby, which she picks up.

"He was here," she says.

"How do you know?" asks Duncan.

She hands him the severed feeding tube and shines the flashlight around the backyard to see if there's any other way out as Duncan tosses the piece of tubing away in disgust, then she walks back around to the street and stands in front of the darkened house.

"What are we doing?" says Duncan.

Shannon holds up a single index finger, hoping Duncan will get the hint.

"Are we playing charades?" he says. "Or are you telling me I'm number one?"

"No," she says, holding up her middle finger with a smile. "That would be this."

"I bet you have taken a dump in front of someone."

Shannon walks over to the middle house, which in addition to being lit up with Christmas lights has several interior lights on, indicating the likelihood that someone's home.

"Let me do the talking," says Shannon as they walk up the path to the house. She points to Duncan's stun baton. "And keep that thing out of sight. I don't want to see it unless you have to use it."

"You know, you're not the first woman who's told me that."

They walk up to the front porch, where Shannon notices an empty chair next to a sack that says SANTA'S

TOYS as she rings the doorbell. A few moments later the front door opens and a woman greets them.

"You got here fast," says the woman. "Oh, I'm sorry. I thought you were the police."

"No, we're just from down the street," says Shannon. "Why, has there been a problem?"

"Oh, just some kids messing with our Christmas decorations," says the woman. "Every year it's something different. Last year they sprayed graffiti on the sleigh. This year they stole Santa."

"They stole Santa?" says Shannon.

"Well his suit, anyway." The woman points to the chair. "They took the mannequin and the stuffing and shoved it into the bushes."

Shannon glances at Duncan, who raises his eyebrows.

"I don't know why my husband insists on putting up all these decorations when people do things like this," says the woman. "But I guess he's just a big kid at heart."

"Aren't we all," says Duncan.

"So how can I help you?" asks the woman.

"We're looking for a lost cat," says Shannon. "It's my daughter's. We're hoping maybe you'd seen it."

"Big guy with white hair," says Duncan. "Answers to Zombie."

"That's an odd name for a cat," says the woman. "But I'm sorry, I haven't seen any cats around here. Not a good place for them to be running loose, if you ask me, what with all of the critters in the woods."

"Well, thanks for your time," says Shannon. "Sorry to bother you."

"Not at all," says the woman. "And good luck finding Zombie."

After the woman closes the door, Duncan reaches into Santa's sack of toys and pulls out a turquoise surgical gown. "Looks like we have a winner," he says. "A zombie dressed up like Santa Claus. I wonder what happens if you end up on the naughty list?"

Shannon turns and walks off the porch as she takes out her cell phone and dials Carter's number to tell him the news.

"Crap," says Duncan from behind her. "I should have asked if I could use their bathroom."

TWELVE

Annie lies curled up asleep on the couch next to me in pink flannel pajamas with black and white bunnies, her head on a small pillow in my lap. The remnants of our dinner sit on the coffee table. Microwaved pesto tortellini and mac and cheese. I was never a big fan of frozen food when I was alive, but after a year of two daily doses of brown goo pumped directly into my stomach through my feeding tube, this tasted like gourmet cooking.

It's now after ten o'clock and I'm getting more comfortable by the moment. I look over at the front window and the darkness floating beyond the venetian blinds and I know that I should get out of here to try to find some help. I've been thinking that for the past several hours, but I can't seem to motivate myself to get off the couch.

That and I don't want to disappoint this little girl who believes I'm Santa Claus.

The Christmas specials ended a while ago, so we watched *Home Alone* and *Elf* before Annie eventually drifted off to sleep. For the past hour or so I've been channel surfing from CNN to CNBC to the local cable channels, searching for any news about a group of zombies that escaped from the research facility. I was hoping to find out where they're looking for us and if the local authorities had alerted the public to be on the lookout, but so far I haven't found anything.

However, I do come across *Zombie Hunters,* a reality program on the Discovery Channel, as well as *World's Wildest Zombie Chases* on Fox—both of which focus on how to catch and properly destroy a zombie. This is a definite change from the reality shows I remember, which had more zombie-positive fare, like *Dancing with the Undead* and *The Real Zombies of Beverly Hills.* And during commercial breaks for both shows, thirty-second PSAs run explaining what to do in the event that anyone encounters a zombie:

1. Make your way to the nearest building.
2. Get inside.
3. Contact the authorities.
4. Refrain from inciting the zombies with abusive language or by throwing expired food products at them.

I don't remember anything like this on television before I was removed from circulation. While I know the push for zombie rights was met with considerable resistance, I'm getting the distinct impression that we're not media darlings anymore.

That and I haven't seen a single commercial for zombie hygiene products.

pine-sol bubble baths
mask the stench of rotting flesh
i smell like christmas

I decide I've spent enough time relaxing and drinking chocolate-flavored high-fructose corn syrup and watching reality television. It's time for me to get out of here and do something a little more proactive.

But I can't just leave Annie on the couch.

I slide out from under her, get to my feet, then pick her up in my arms and carry her into her bedroom, taking short, measured steps to make sure my legs don't give out on me.

I look down at her and for a moment I see my own daughter when she was just six years old, one hand curled up beneath her chin, a faint smile at the corners of her mouth as I carry her to bed and kiss her good night on the forehead.

"I love you, Annie," I say.

"I love you, too, Daddy."

The problem with remembering what it was like to be human is that it reminds you about the limitations of your current existence.

Back in the present I set Annie down on her bed and pull the covers up over her. Before I realize what I'm doing, I lean down to kiss her good night on the forehead.

She opens her eyes and giggles. "Your beard tickles."

I almost open my mouth to say *I love you,* but then I catch myself. "Thanks for the hot chocolate and cookies, Annie."

"You're welcome," she says, looking so cute I could just eat her up. Euphemistically, of course.

I look down at Annie, my paternal instincts slamming into me, creating a strong desire to stay and protect her. Which I know is somewhat of a paradox considering that I'm technically the monster. Still, part of me doesn't want to go and I'm starting to get a little choked up.

"Merry Christmas, Annie," I say.

As I turn to leave, I hear her voice behind me. "You're leaving?"

I turn around to find her sitting up in bed, looking at me like she's lost her only friend in the world.

"I'm afraid so," I say.

"Do you have to go?"

She isn't making this any easier.

"I have to get back to the North Pole," I say, trying to stay in character. "I still have a lot of work to do before Christmas."

Out on the television, someone is saying that if you encounter a zombie on the street, don't run into a shopping mall.

"Can you stay with me for a little while longer?" She's still staring at me with her wounded expression. "Just a few more minutes? Please?"

I open my mouth to tell her that I can't, that I have to get going, but the words die in my throat.

"Okay." I walk over to her bed. "But only for a few more minutes."

Annie scoots over while I lie down on top of the covers next to her. She curls up against me and I glance over to see her looking at me, wearing that cute little smile of hers, and I'm pretty much melting into a puddle of zombie.

"Can you tell me a story?" she asks. "Something about Christmas, with reindeer and elves and winter warlocks?"

I try to think of some story to tell her that includes all those things but I can't think of anything.

"How about 'The Night Before Christmas' instead?" I say.

She gets this look on her face like she's thinking it over and then finally gives a single, emphatic nod.

"I'm okay with that."

"Good to know. You ready?"

Annie moves around and adjusts herself under the covers, then settles in again next to me. "Ready."

"Okay," I say, trying to remember how this goes. " 'Twas the night before Christmas, when all through the house, not a creature was stirring, not even a mouse."

"I like mice," says Annie, pressing her face into my shoulder. "They're cute."

"The stockings were hung by the chimney with care, in hopes that St. Nicholas soon would be there."

"Yay! That's you."

"The children were nestled all snug in their beds, while visions of sugar plums danced in their heads."

"What's a sugar plum?"

"I believe it's a piece of dried fruit."

Annie makes a face. "Yuck. That doesn't sound like a vision I want dancing around in my head."

"I don't blame you. What would you rather have?"

She thinks on this for a moment, furrowing her brow. "How about candy canes?"

"Good choice," I say. "While visions of candy canes danced in their heads."

"That's a lot better."

"And Ma in her kerchief and I in my cap, had just settled down for a long winter's nap."

"What kind of cap?"

"You know, if you're going to keep interrupting, we're never going to get to the end of the story."

"I can't help it. I have questions and I want answers."

"A nightcap. They used to wear them in the old days."

"How old?"

"Before you were born," I say. "When out on the lawn there arose such a clatter . . ."

I tell her the rest of the poem, though I don't know all of it by heart and I have to make up some of it; still, I know enough to make it work. Annie helps me to fill in all the other details so that by the end of it, we've managed to work in elves and winter warlocks and Frosty the Snowman. Even Heat Miser and Snow Miser get a cameo. The reindeer, of course, were already part of the story. Even stupid Rudolph, whom Annie now seems to have a beef with for kicking me.

"Thanks, Santa," she says around a yawn. "I think I'm ready to go to sleep now."

"That sounds like a good idea," I say as I get out of bed. It's now nearly eleven and I realize Annie's mom isn't home yet, which is good for me but not so much for Annie. I almost want to take her with me, but I know that would be a bad idea. First of all, she's not my daughter. And second, I'm not alive, which would complicate the adoption process.

"Good night, Annie."

"Wait!" she says. "You haven't asked me what I want for Christmas."

"Where are my manners?" I say. "So what would you like for Christmas?"

"Not like that. I'm supposed to sit on your lap."

"Oh, right." I sit back down on the bed and Annie gets out from beneath the covers and climbs aboard. I'm never getting out of here. "How's that?" I ask.

"That's better," she says.

I clear my throat. "And what would you like for Christmas, Annie?"

She giggles. Then the laughter dissipates and she gets this pensive expression. I'm expecting her to tell me she wants a dollhouse or an iPod or a pair of roller skates, and she simply can't make up her mind. Maybe she even wants something as extravagant as a laptop.

Instead, she looks at me and declares:

"I'd like my mother to spend more time with me."

I stare back at her sitting on my lap, looking up at me with her serious face, and I don't know what to say. I can't promise this, not even if I were the real Santa. It's not something one can put in a box and wrap with a bow or stuff into her stocking, even if she had one.

"I know that's not something you can make in your workshop, but I thought I'd ask, just in case," she says, being very understanding for a nine-year-old. "So if you can't, then I guess I'd just like a big stuffed panda bear."

I don't know why I say it. Maybe it's because of the expression on her face. Or the way she put those little marshmallows in my hot chocolate. Or the fact that she's home alone a few days before Christmas without a tree or a stocking or her mother.

"I'll see what I can do."

Annie throws her arms around me and gives me a big hug. "Thank you, Santa. You're the best."

I hug her back and wonder what the hell I've gotten myself into.

THIRTEEN

"Hey, Santa baby!"

"Merry Christmas, Santa!"

"Santa, we love you!"

I'm walking through downtown Portland just past midnight and waving to my adoring public. It's a bit of a change from the insults I used to get when I went for a walk. Most of the time people would call me a brain-dead abortion and pelt me with expired food products or call Animal Control, so anything that doesn't result in me getting dismembered or thrown into a cage is like winning the lottery.

It stopped snowing before I left Annie's and most of the snow has already melted, but the air is cold and the streets are slick. I continue past closed shops and banks and restaurants and the occasional bar filled with pre-holiday revelers, thinking about how I'm going to keep the promises I made to Annie while searching for some fellow zombies. But I'm not having any luck on either count.

I know there have to be some zombies around here somewhere. The population density and the preponderance of homeless provide both a cover and a constant food supply, so zombies typically take to urban centers like piranhas to a drowning cow. However, it is past curfew, which means most zombies will tend to make themselves scarce. And if the television programming I've seen is any indication of the state of zombie tolerance, getting picked up by Animal Control is the least of our worries. As I've learned firsthand, nothing good happens to zombies after midnight.

The good news is, my legs are beginning to become used to the idea of walking again and I feel steadier on my feet, but it still took me more than an hour to walk here from Annie's. The bad news is, although my legs are regaining some of their strength, I'm starting to feel a little stiff. Not just in my legs, but all over. A subtle thickening that seems to affect my arms and legs and chest.

While I didn't experience it before I reanimated, since it tends to occur within the first few hours after death, I'd almost swear that I was suffering from rigor mortis.

Plus I think I might be lactose intolerant.

muscles become stiff
stomach starts to bloat and cramp
too much hot cocoa

After another couple of blocks, the Santa groupies have found their way into bars or cabs and I'm alone on the street, wondering what's going on with me and where the other zombies are and just how the hell I'm going to grant Annie's Christmas wish.

I'm so preoccupied with my thoughts that I don't notice the figure walking along behind me in the shadows until I hear him whistle.

I look back and see him less than a block away, wearing a dark sweatshirt and a baseball cap. Something tells me he's not the Welcome Wagon, so I cut over to Park Avenue and cross to the pedestrian median, looking for a bench or a tree or a shrub to hide behind, when I hear another whistle and two other figures come out of the shadows on either side of me.

I turn to look for a place to run, but running still isn't my strong suit. I'm more of a stumble-and-stagger kind of guy. So before I can do much of anything, they've got me surrounded.

Two of them are wearing hoodies, obscuring their faces, while the third one who comes up behind me is wearing a Boston Red Sox cap. I don't see any stun batons, so I'm guessing they're not from the research facility, which means they're probably just Breathers out looking for trouble. Fraternity boys or gang members or bored teenagers on Christmas break. Fortunately they don't know I'm a zombie.

"Ho ho ho," I bellow, hoping to disarm them with my Santa charm. "Merry Christmas!"

"Fuck Christmas," the one in the Red Sox hat says with a South Boston accent.

The one on my right lets out a nervous giggle.

"Shut your trap, Mykle," says South Boston, who looks left and right. "You two sure he's alone?"

"Yes, but I don't know for how long," says the one on my left. "Are you sure this is a good idea?"

"For fuck's sake, Cameron," says South Boston. "Will you stop whining?"

"Yeah, Cameron," says Mykle. "For fuck's sake."

After a moment, South Boston takes a step closer so that I can see his face. He has a scruff of a goatee on his chin and piercings in his nose and left eyebrow that appear to be infected. "So what's St. Nick doing out all alone after midnight?"

"Just making my list and checking it twice," I say, trying to figure out how I can turn this to my advantage, but at the moment, every way I turn seems to lead to a dead end.

"Have you found out who's naughty or nice?" says Mykle with a giggle.

"Hey," says South Boston. "I thought I said to shut your trap."

"Sorry, Jeff," says Mykle.

The fact that they're not worried about giving their names either means that they don't plan on leaving any witnesses or else they're not particularly bright.

I've got my money on not particularly bright.

"Well, I'm happy to say you've all made the nice list," I say, trying to buy some time. "Just in case you were worried."

"We're not worried," says South Boston/Jeff, who

takes another step forward as the other two follow his lead and close in. "But *you* should be."

So much for my boring night. I look left and right, expecting them to make their move and hoping I can somehow manage to bite one of them, but instead they just stand there surrounding me in a threatening posture as if they're waiting for something. Cameron, the one on my left wearing wire-rim glasses, reaches up and scratches at his nose while Mykle, the one on my right, lets out another nervous laugh.

"So how do we go about this?" says Cameron.

"I don't know," says Mykle. "I thought Jeff knew what to do."

Jeff avoids eye contact and scratches his forehead. "Ah, for fuck's sake."

I look around at the three of them and wonder what the hell is going on. It occurs to me that they haven't flashed any weapons. I also notice all three of them are paler than your average Breather and that Mykle has several deep, open wounds on his face. And none of them exactly smells like Irish Spring.

It takes me another moment to figure it out. And when I do, I start to laugh, which I haven't done in so long I've forgotten how good it feels.

"What the fuck's so funny?" asks Jeff.

I glance at all three of them, wondering how long they've been zombies. "You guys are kind of new at this, aren't you?"

The three of them look back and forth at each other as if I'd just told them one in three men has had a homosexual experience and they're all trying to figure out which one of them it is.

"How can you tell?" asks Cameron.

"Don't admit it," says Jeff.

"He already knows," says Cameron. "What's the point?"

"The point is we don't want to look like douche bags," says Jeff.

Mykle lets out a snort. "I think it's too late for that."

No one says anything, so I figure this is a good time for show and tell.

"If it makes you feel any better," I say, unbuttoning my coat to show off my chopped-off feeding tube, "I'm not a Breather, either."

Several moments of awkward silence pass. It's so quiet I can hear someone's stomach growling. Either that or their abdominal cavity is about to burst open.

"Well," says Mykle, "so much for dinner."

FOURTEEN

The four of us are gathered in the basement beneath a dry cleaners owned by Jeff's older sister. Jeff and I sit on folding beach chairs, which—in addition to a mattress, a couple of sleeping bags, a folding card table, a mini-refrigerator, a coffeemaker, a dozen cases of diet soda, several gallons of Pine-Sol, and a microwave—account for the basement's decor.

I've already given them the CliffsNotes version of what happened to me and how I ended up here dressed in a Santa Claus suit, though I left out the part about Annie. Somehow I don't think they'd understand.

"That's harsh what they did to you," says Jeff. "I wouldn't wish that shit on a Yankees fan."

Jeff grew up in South Boston but moved here a couple of years ago. He died in October on his twenty-seventh birthday when he drove off the side of the Columbia River Highway after a night of shooting pool and drinking at the McMenamins in Troutdale. His younger sister, Heather, was riding shotgun and ended up in a coma.

Sounds familiar. Only I wasn't drinking or playing pool, but just nodded off. And my wife, who was riding shotgun, never woke up, either. So both Jeff and I carry around some of the same unpacked baggage.

"Biggest mistake of my life," says Jeff.

"And your death," says Mykle.

"*Death* isn't the proper terminology," says Cameron, adjusting his glasses like Clark Kent. "Technically, we're undead."

"Fuck technically," says Jeff.

"Yeah," says Mykle. "Why do you have to correct everyone?"

"I'm not correcting," says Cameron. "I'm just clarifying."

"Well, you clarify *a lot*," says Mykle.

Cameron was a thirty-two-year-old linguistics professor at Portland State until he choked to death on a stack of double blueberry pancakes at IHOP.

"Forty-seven people in the restaurant at the time and no one knew the Heimlich maneuver," he says. "Now every time I burp or fart it smells like blueberries."

"At least your pancakes didn't have claws," says Mykle.

Mykle, a zoology undergrad at Oregon State, was attacked and killed by a black bear as he was hiking near Multnomah Falls in the Columbia River Gorge.

Nothing like a side of irony to go with your serving of unwanted afterlife.

"That must have hurt," I say to Mykle.

"You have no idea," he says, fingering the claw wounds on his face.

While we continue to get acquainted, Cameron finishes heating up some Hot Pockets in the microwave as Mykle sits on a mattress drinking some Pine-Sol and thumbing through a battered copy of *The Zombie Survival Guide.*

Somehow I don't think he's going to find anything useful in there.

Both Cameron and Mykle became zombies within the past month, which makes Jeff the most senior member of the trio. Fortunately they were all embalmed prior to reanimating, which cuts down on the speed of decomposition. And while you can postpone the inevitable by getting formaldehyde fixes from diet sodas, cosmetics, shampoos, and household cleaners, without a steady diet of Breather your average zombie will last about six months.

And none of them has eaten Breather.

"What's it taste like?" asks Cameron, handing me a Hot Pocket. "Breather?"

All three of them stare at me, waiting for my answer like I'm the Dalai Lama and they've just asked me the meaning of life.

I take a bite of my Hot Pocket. "Well, I guess that all depends on how you choose to cook it."

An easy way to prepare Breather is to pat it dry on a paper towel, then sauté in butter in a large, heavy skillet over moderately high heat 4–5 minutes until lightly browned. Sprinkle with salt and pepper and serve with lemon over white rice.

"What's your favorite way to eat it?" asks Mykle.

"Breather tastes good no matter how you prepare it," I say. "But my favorite is probably barbecued ribs."

Wrap ribs in double-thickness heavy foil and bake 1½ hours at 350 degrees. Unwrap and marinate in sauce 1–2 hours at room temperature, then broil 20 minutes over a moderate coal fire. Feeds 6 zombies.

All this talk about eating Breather is making me salivate, though I notice that I'm feeling a little queasy and I wonder if my stomach is having trouble adjusting to all the solid food I've consumed since my escape. Either that or this Hot Pocket is past its expiration date.

But then, aren't we all?

Cameron, Mykle, and Jeff keep asking me questions about eating Breather and what it was like for me when I first reanimated. How people treated me. Where I lived. What I did for fun. So I tell them everything. The SPCA. My parents. Undead Anonymous.

"Undead Anonymous?" says Jeff. "What's that?"

"A support group for zombies. It's where we meet other zombies and learn how to deal with being undead," I say, thinking about Rita and Jerry and everyone else. "You don't have a chapter here in Portland?"

Jeff shakes his head.

"I don't think Undead Anonymous exists anymore," says Cameron.

"Yeah, it doesn't say anything in here about zombie support groups," says Mykle, flipping through *The Zombie*

Survival Guide. "Just a bunch of stuff about weapons and supplies and crap like that. Why the hell would a zombie need a flamethrower?"

"That's not a survival guide for zombies," says Cameron. "It's a survival guide for Breathers to protect themselves *from* zombies. In other words, from us."

"Really?" Mykle looks at the cover, then tosses the book aside. "Well, that's lame."

"What do you mean Undead Anonymous doesn't exist anymore?" I ask. "Where do zombies go for support?"

"I think a lot has changed since you've been gone," says Cameron.

And Cameron starts talking.

After the events of last New Year's Eve, civil rights for zombies became a real movement. Zombies across the nation started committing acts of civil disobedience, organizing demonstrations, instigating riots. A lot of Breathers died, which didn't sit well with society at large. As a result, faster than you could say "Patriot Act," Congress passed the Reanimant Mandate, which was written up and pushed through the House and the Senate in a matter of weeks. Even the ACLU, the NAACP, and Amnesty International were on board.

Simply put, the new world order called for the destruction of any newly reanimated corpse. All zombies were now considered hazardous to every living American. Any chance of equality went up in a cloud of bipartisan smoke. If being a zombie was a crappy existence before, then it's a pile of shit now.

I listen as Cameron continues to explain just how high the pile has grown.

Any existing zombies under the care of family members or other legal guardians had to be turned over to the state for processing, no exceptions. Most ended up in research facilities or donated to medical science or used as crash test dummies. Others—the unlucky ones—got shipped off to zombie zoos or imprisoned on a handful of zombie reality television programs. The rest ended up destroyed or in designated zombie landfills.

But not everyone played follow the leader. A number of zombies went underground, aided by Breathers sympathetic to their used-to-be husbands, wives, siblings, friends, and children. They sought refuge in basements and rental units and abandoned buildings. They blended in with homeless populations and traveling circuses and Burning Man communities.

Breathers who are sympathetic to the plight of the undead risk their own personal freedom at the hands of local and federal law enforcement, since harboring or aiding and abetting a zombie is now considered a federal crime. Jeff's older sister, Rose, provides the use of the dry cleaners basement to her brother in direct disregard of the Reanimant Mandate—a transgression that could land her in prison for three to five years.

Cameron wasn't kidding when he said a lot has changed. The only thing my parents had to worry about by keeping me in their wine cellar was how it affected the property values.

"So there's not any 'zombie community' left to speak

of," says Cameron. "Without anyone to help us, we're all pretty much screwed."

I get the feeling Cameron's not exactly a glass-half-full kind of guy.

"So you guys are on your own?" I say. "With no one to help you?"

The three of them either shrug or shake their heads.

"So what do you say?" says Jeff.

"What do I say about what?" I say.

"About helping us," says Jeff.

"Helping you with what?"

"To become better zombies," he says. "After all, you're kind of a zombie advisor and in case you haven't noticed, we're not exactly honor roll students here."

I look at Mykle, who fingers his claw marks until part of his face peels off, while Cameron cleans his glasses and gives a sheepish smile.

"It would mean a lot to us if you could show us the ropes," says Jeff.

"Yeah," says Mykle. "Show us the ropes."

I look at the three of them and wonder if I was like this. Inept and clueless and completely unprepared for my undeath. I'd like to think I had a better handle on how to deal with the challenges of being a zombie, but it seems like I've always known how to do what I do. Though I probably never would have found my purpose had it not been for Helen and Ray.

I guess even zombies need a little guidance.

"Okay," I say. "So where do you want to start?"

FIFTEEN

I'm standing in front of one of the basement walls, upon which I've used a black Sharpie to draw two crude renditions of a human silhouette, one facing forward and the other facing to the side. I've left off the relevant body parts identifying them as either male or female. This isn't a Human Sexuality class. I'm not teaching my fellow zombies about reproduction. What I'm doing is giving them a crash course in How to Eat Breather.

Not exactly something they taught us in Undead Anonymous, but I'm just doing my best to give them some practical applications for the twenty-first-century zombie.

Jeff, Mykle, and Cameron sit in beach chairs on the floor at my feet, all three of them wearing earnest and attentive expressions. Cameron's even taking notes.

"So can you eat Breather raw?" asks Mykle. "You know, like sushi?"

In a medium bowl, combine 2 pounds of fresh cubed Breather, 1 cup soy sauce, ¾ cup chopped green onions,

2 tablespoons sesame oil, and 1 tablespoon toasted sesame seeds. Refrigerate for 2 hours before serving.

"You can," I say. "But it's a little chewy. Personally I always preferred mine medium to medium-rare. That way you lock in the flavor without sacrificing tenderness. Plus Breather tends to be full of germs and parasites, so it's best to cook it for a few minutes so you don't end up with worms."

"What's it like?" asks Cameron. "Eating Breather?"

While he's not saying it outright, I detect the moral and ethical implications inherent in Cameron's question.

You'd think eating humans would be second nature for a zombie. But eating human flesh isn't something your average zombie knows how to do once the umbilical cord to life has been cut. Cannibalism is cannibalism, whether you're undead or alive, and the idea takes some getting used to. It's not so much an issue of developing a taste for it, because Breather tastes yummy. It's more a question of learning how to accept your reality—lock, stock, and smoked Breather.

I was fortunate enough to be introduced to the joys of human flesh without knowing what I was eating, so I warmed up to it without having to deal with some of the questions that come with making such a significant shift in ideology.

Is this ethical?

Am I a bad zombie?

Would this taste better with ketchup or barbecue sauce?

On some level, I always knew what I was eating,

which made it easier for me to stomach the truth once I admitted it to myself. However, not everyone has the option of lying to themselves until they're ready to embrace their true nature.

"It's easier than you might think," I say, answering Cameron's question. "If you're just starting out, you might want to eat it in a sandwich or with a couple of sides, as there can be a bit of an adjustment period. Especially if you were a vegetarian."

While some manage to make the transition, most vegetarians don't do well as zombies, especially if they were militant about not eating meat. And if you were a full-on vegan, you might as well forget it. Just douse yourself in gasoline and light yourself on fire and get it over with.

"What are the best parts to eat?" asks Jeff.

"It's all good," I say. "And a good zombie never wastes any food. But the most tender parts include the ribs and the loin."

On the figures I've drawn on the wall, I've done my best to outline the different parts of the human body and I point to the relevant areas of my drawings to demonstrate.

"Age and exercise is what tends to toughen up Breathers," I say, "especially when it comes to the legs, shoulders, and the butt. So when hunting Breathers, it's a good idea to stay away from gyms and retirement communities."

Cameron scribbles in his notebook as Mykle raises his hand. "What about the breasts?"

"Are you talking male or female?" I ask.

"Female," he says, with a snort. Either he's blushing or he died facedown and all the blood pooled in his face.

"Breasts are mostly fatty tissue," I say, "so there's not much point in eating them. Unless you have a fetish."

We talk some more about cooking methods and the best way to freeze uncooked or uneaten portions. Your average 190-pound Breather male can feed a single zombie for ten days to two weeks, depending on your portion sizes and how often you snack between meals. Even with the three of them sharing, it'll most likely take a good three days to get through a single John or Jane. I suggest they invest in a small chest freezer or something that can hold up to fifty pounds of meat.

"It'll help to cut down on spoilage," I say. "I don't know how your sister feels about rotting human flesh, but most Breathers aren't big fans of the smell."

"No kidding," says Jeff. "She's already started carrying a spray can of air freshener whenever she comes down here. Which doesn't happen that often anymore. She used to come down every day to check on me. Now I'm lucky if I see her twice a week."

I can hear the disappointment in Jeff's voice and I understand how he feels. It's not easy when you discover that your friends and family can't stand the smell of you or the thought of being around you anymore. But that's what happens. That's the inevitability of our existence. To be shunned and despised and abhorred.

After a while, you just get used to it.

"Here's something else you all need to know," I say. "And this might be the most important thing you need to remember."

Mykle and Jeff watch me attentively while Cameron prepares a fresh sheet in his notebook.

"As much as you want to believe that your sister or your parents or your loved ones still feel the same about you as they did when you were alive, you have to realize that you don't have anything in common with them anymore, and eventually they're going to realize the same thing. When that happens, the moment they decide that you've become more trouble than you're worth, no amount of love or memories or familial obligation is going to matter."

Cameron has stopped taking notes and is now watching me intently along with Jeff and Mykle.

"You can't count on the living to protect you," I say. "I know it's easier to pretend that everything is going to stay the same, but sooner or later you're going to have to admit that the only ones you're going to be able to count on are yourselves."

No one really wants to face the truth about what it's like to be a zombie, especially when the life you used to live is still going on all around you. But all you can do is sit and watch your old life happen. You're no longer a participant. You're just a spectator.

"The illusion is that somehow you're still a part of the life you once had," I say. "Once you realize that your old existence has forsaken you, once you embrace the truth of your new existence, that's when you can start to own it. That's when your true undeath begins."

The three of them are nodding, as if what I've said is absorbing into their gradually liquefying brains and striking a chord.

"That's what I'm talking about," says Jeff. "This is exactly what we need."

Cameron and Mykle continue nodding their agreement.

"Will you stay with us?" asks Cameron. "Teach us everything you know? Be our spiritual guide?"

"Yeah," says Mykle. "Like the Dolly Momma?"

"I think you mean the Dalai Lama," says Cameron.

"Whatever, Sir Correct-A-Lot."

The idea of staying anyplace seems like a bad idea, but at the moment I don't have a lot of options for relocation. Not until I rescue Patrick and keep my promise to Annie.

And I still have no idea how I'm going to do either.

"If I agree to stay," I say, "will the three of you help me with something?"

"Lay it out," says Jeff.

I tell them everything about Patrick and how he helped me to escape and how he ended up getting caught for his efforts. As for Annie, that's something I'll have to figure out on my own.

"I have to go back and try to rescue Patrick," I say. "And as many of the others as I can, but I can't do it alone. And I can't promise we won't all end up getting caught and thrown into cages and used for medical research. So there's that."

The three of them sit there contemplating for a few moments before they answer.

"I'm in," says Jeff.

"Me too," says Mykle.

"I don't know," says Cameron. "It sounds kind of risky."

"We're zombies," says Jeff. "Walking out the fuckin' door is risky."

"Yeah, Cam," says Mykle. "Come on."

After a moment, Cameron says, "Okay," then he looks from Jeff to Mykle to me. "But are the four of us going to be enough?"

"I don't know," I say. "If we had a couple more bodies that would help. Are there any other zombies around we could ask?"

"Not really," says Jeff. "Most of the others make themselves scarce. And those that are around tend to have major trust issues."

"What about the Creep Brothers?" says Mykle.

"Who are the Creep Brothers?" I say.

"They're these two zombies we see around every now and then," says Cameron. "But I doubt if they'd be any help."

"Why not?" I ask.

"Because they're creepy," says Mykle.

"Creepy in what way?" I ask.

"In every fuckin' way," says Jeff.

"For one thing, they never say anything," says Cameron. "They just smile and giggle and run away whenever they see us."

"And they hum a lot," says Mykle.

"They hum?" I say. "What do you mean, they hum?"

"Songs," says Cameron. "Melodies. Show tunes. They hum together in perfect harmony like they're listening to the same song."

"They're kind of creepy," says Mykle.

"Do you know where they are?" I ask.

"I think they're squatting in some place on West Burnside over by the Jade Mermaid Tattoo Parlor," says Jeff.

"Okay then," I say, standing up. "Let's go recruiting."

SIXTEEN

Shannon sits in a chair in Carter's office looking out the window at the parking lot two stories below, the halogen lamps lighting up every square inch of the asphalt in the early morning darkness. Half a dozen cars sit in scattered parking spaces, their hoods and roofs and windshields dusted with snow. Beyond the parking lot stands the ten-foot-high wooden fence topped with razor wire running along the perimeter of the body farm.

Behind her, Carter talks into his cell phone.

"You have no idea where it might be?" he says.

She can't hear the response to Carter's question, but apparently it's not to his satisfaction.

"That would be the most likely scenario," says Carter. "So thank you for pointing out the obvious."

For the past eight hours, Carter had his Recovery teams and Animal Control searching the perimeter neighborhoods and sweeping the area between OHSU and downtown Portland. The only St. Nicks they found were of the Rent-A-Santa variety and all of them were human.

"Keep me updated," says Carter. "And let's try to avoid any lawsuits, shall we?"

Apparently, a couple of the boys in Recovery roughed up a Salvation Army Santa who they thought was a zombie, but it turned out he was just an aging hippie who hadn't bathed in several days.

Carter presses END on the phone and brings up the feed from the kennel on one of the video monitors in his office. He replays the video of the escape, watching as the zombies file out of the room. Shannon notices that Andy turns and waves to someone out of frame before he makes his escape.

"Damn zombie sympathizers," says Carter. "They're a bigger headache than the animal rights groups."

Carter ends the video playback and a live feed from the kennel plays on his monitor, showing most of the cages occupied. He stares at the monitor, stroking his mustache, whatever he's thinking hidden behind his calm, emotionless expression.

"I want to know if any of the other Reanimants have information that can help us," he says. "Any of them who saw it or who knows which way it went. I want Bob in here as soon as he can to get on it."

"What exactly do you want Bob to do?" asks Shannon.

Carter gives her a small, humorless smile. "I want him to do whatever is necessary."

Shannon looks up at the monitor and pretends not to feel anything.

"And first thing in the morning, I want you and Duncan out there again looking for it," says Carter. "This time check basements, garages, shopping malls. Any possible hiding place. Knock on doors. Ask questions. Find out if anyone's seen a stray Santa wandering around. Animal Control and the police will be out with cadaver dogs, but I don't trust any of them. So I'm trusting you."

Carter stares at her with that same lack of expression that often makes her wonder if he's skilled at hiding his emotions or if he's just a borderline sociopath.

"Thank you," she says, because she knows that's what he wants to hear.

"Unfortunately we may not have the luxury of time." Carter walks over to his desk and removes a plastic syringe filled with a dark brown fluid. "It's already missed a full day of feedings. If the aversion therapy it's been undergoing has started working, then it's not going to be able to feed itself and will reject any attempt at eating human flesh. And without the genetically altered supplements we've been giving it for the past year, the decomposition process will likely start within twenty-four hours. It won't be able to survive. Which means the longer it's out there, the more damage will be done. More than two or three days and all of our work might be lost."

Shannon tries to imagine what it's like to feel the effects of decomposition, to experience rigor mortis and bloat and putrefaction and be aware of what's happening to you, to know that you're rotting inside. A shiver runs through her in a single body spasm.

"This will help to temporarily reverse any damage." Carter walks over to Shannon and hands her the syringe. "The effects will likely only last four to six hours, but that should give us the time we need to get back on track."

Shannon pockets the syringe as Carter walks over to the window and stares out at the body farm.

"Find it," he says. "Whatever you do, find it and bring it back."

SEVENTEEN

The four of us are walking behind the First Presbyterian Church, heading toward the elevated portion of the 405 freeway. We've been walking around for the better part of an hour checking alleys and parking lots and deserted buildings without any sign of the Creep Brothers.

"Hey," says Mykle. "Do you guys think you'd survive the zombie apocalypse?"

"In case you haven't noticed," says Jeff, "we *are* the zombie apocalypse."

"I wouldn't exactly call us an apocalypse," says Cameron. "More like an ongoing issue . . ."

I haven't mentioned anything to the others, but I've noticed that my legs are starting to feel heavier, like someone has turned up the gravity. And it's not just my legs but my arms and hands, too. Like my blood has stopped circulating and is starting to settle in my extremities. I've never experienced hypostasis before, so I don't know if that's what's happening to me, but I definitely feel weird.

blood pools and settles
postmortem lividity
i could use a hug

I'm guessing most Hollywood zombies don't have to deal with problems like this.

"Maybe it would be better if we split up," says Jeff. "The Creep Brothers might be more likely to approach one of us if we're alone rather than in a group."

"I don't think that's a good idea," says Cameron.

"You don't think anything's a good idea," says Mykle.

"I'm just cautious by nature," says Cameron.

"More like a douche bag by nature," says Mykle.

In spite of Cameron's misgivings, we decide to each head off in a different direction to try to find the Creep Brothers.

"If anyone sees anything," says Jeff, "just whistle."

"What if we see a Breather?" asks Cameron.

"Then whistle twice."

"What if we see Animal Control?" says Mykle.

"Jesus, I don't know," says Jeff. "Then whistle fuckin' *Andy Griffith*."

Mykle scrunches his clawed-up face in concentration. "I forget how that goes."

I head off alone while Mykle asks Cameron to whistle the theme song to *The Andy Griffith Show* and Jeff tells him to shut the fuck up.

How these three have managed to make it a month without getting destroyed is a mystery.

There's no one else out on the streets and other than

my own footsteps the only sound I hear is the occasional hum of tires on asphalt from the cars racing past overhead on the 405 freeway.

I don't see or hear any sign of the Creep Brothers, so I keep walking, paying attention to the way my body continues to grow heavy and take on a sluggish quality that makes me feel like I'm walking in mud. Whatever is going on with me, I think I need to find something to eat soon. And I'm not talking about a Hot Pocket or frozen pesto tortellini.

I'd faddle and I'd fiddle
Fat fry you on the griddle
Sautéing your remains
On your flesh I'd be snackin'
And your skull I would be crackin'
If I only had some brains

It's the first time I've sung the lyrics out loud and it makes the song that much more cathartic. So I keep singing, softly at first, then a little bit louder. After a few minutes, someone starts whistling the tune on my left. When I look that direction, the whistling cuts off and continues on my right without missing a note. At first I think it's Mykle or Cameron or Jeff playing around, but then I realize they're probably not that musically talented.

The whistling goes back and forth like this for the entire song, drawing closer, surrounding me, but I still don't see anyone. Then I hear the last part of the song in stereo, in perfect harmony. When it finishes, I see two figures standing on either side of me in the shadows less than ten feet away, dressed in dark green tights and turtlenecks, just staring. I can't clearly see their faces but I'm guessing I've found my recruits.

The Creep Brothers approach me, taking perfectly timed steps in sync with one another as if they were a Cirque du Soleil team performing a routine. Then they stop a few feet away and smile like a couple of Cheshire cats.

And I can't believe my eyes.

Although I haven't seen them since the events of last New Year's Eve, I'd know those smiles anywhere.

I give a huge grin back and wait to see their faces light up with recognition, until I realize they probably don't recognize me with my hair and beard and my Santa Claus getup.

"Zack. Luke," I say, taking off my hat. "It's me. It's Andy."

They both look at me and cock their heads like a couple of dogs that just heard a familiar word they're trying to work out. I know I don't look like I did the last time they saw me, and they seem to have become a little more feral over the past twelve months, but I'm hoping they recognize my voice.

"Andy?" they say in unison, their voices going up a notch on the second syllable.

I nod and try to think of something that will let them know I'm really who I say I am, some shared memory or experience about Ray or going to Sigma Chi to get Tom's arm back, but before I can come up with anything, they close the remaining distance and start sniffing me, beginning at my head and continuing all the way down to my feet. When they stand back up on either side of me, they don't say anything, but I can see from their expressions that they recognize my scent. If they had tails, they'd be wagging.

The next moment, they're both hugging me, their arms wrapped around me and their faces pressed against my shoulders.

"Hey, okay guys," I say. "It's good to see you, too."

EIGHTEEN

Zack and Luke are staying in a room on the third floor of a condemned apartment building on Couch Street, complete with cockroaches and mold growing on the walls and a hibachi grill on the fire escape. When it comes to interior decorating, the twins subscribe to the zombie minimalist school of thinking. Other than a single blanket, a pair of hiking backpacks, and a large bucket in the corner, there's nothing else in the room.

I can see why they picked this place. Not only is it roomy and airy, but it comes with a good view and multiple exits.

While a basement offers more seclusion and privacy and the ability to keep cooler in hot weather, you're kind of limited in your escape routes. Only one way in and one way out. So as soon as the Zombie Patrol finds you, you're pretty much on your way to a composting farm. Plus when you're a decomposing corpse in a basement, lack of air circulation can become a problem so you have to worry more about deodorizers and air fresheners.

Unless, of course, you enjoy the smell of your own hydrogen sulfide.

"Jesus, Mykle," says Jeff, waving the air in front of his face. "Was that you?"

"Not me," says Mykle, taking a sniff. "It smells kind of like blueberries."

They both look at Cameron, who turns a deeper shade of bluish pale. "Sorry. I've been fighting off this latest case of bloat, but it seems like a losing battle."

Although I've never had to deal with bloat, I know what it's like to struggle with your self-confidence. After all, I used to be the poster child for zombies before I started eating Breather.

"Maybe we can do something about that." I turn to Zack and Luke, who sit on either side of me like zombie bookends. "Do you have anything for our friends to eat? And they're virgins, so maybe something less identifiable?"

The two of them get up and scamper off through a doorway on the other side of the room without a word.

"Are you sure about those two?" asks Cameron.

"I think they're kind of cool," says Mykle.

"Definitely not big conversationalists," says Jeff.

Neither of the twins has said much since our reunion. When I asked them what they were doing in Portland, Zack pointed at me while Luke said, "Looking for you."

Which is probably one of the sweetest things I've ever heard.

"I wouldn't worry about them," I say. "They're as loyal

a pair of zombies as you'll find. When it comes to doing what needs to be done, they'll do it. No questions asked."

They were the best personal assistants a celebrity zombie could ask for.

A moment later, the twins return with a gallon-sized Ziploc bag filled with what appears to be beef jerky.

Whenever I see a Ziploc bag, I can't help but think of my parents.

Zack opens the bag and offers the contents to Mykle, Cameron, and Jeff, who each take out a single piece of jerky.

Jeff holds the jerky beneath his nose and sniffs. "Is this what I think it is?"

"It's probably a good idea not to think about it," I say. "Not at first. It cuts down on the gag reflex."

All three of them hold their pieces of jerky up in front of their faces as if trying to make up their minds about what to do. While it's one thing to accept the idea that you're a reanimated corpse, once you eat Breather, it's a slippery slope to losing what's left of your humanity.

"And it'll keep us from decomposing?" asks Cameron.

I take a piece from the bag and point to the twins, who look so human they could probably get a job at Starbucks. "They've been undead for over a year and a half."

The three of them look at Zack and Luke, who offer up matching grins before biting off a mouthful of Breather jerky.

"Good enough for me," says Mykle, then he takes a bite and starts chewing.

Jeff follows suit. Moments later, both he and Mykle are making sounds of ecstasy like they're in a bad porno.

Cameron looks at his piece of jerky, then at Jeff and Mykle, who are each biting off another piece of Breather. After looking at the twins, who are already licking their fingers clean, he looks once at me. Then he closes his eyes and tears off a chunk and follows everyone else down the path of no return.

I watch all of them, my new little family of reanimated corpses, wondering how long we'll be together, then I take a bite of my Breather jerky.

I immediately notice something's wrong. The flavor isn't rapturous the way I remember. It's almost rancid, and I wonder if the jerky has been sitting around for too long and has somehow gone bad. Except no one else seems to be having the same reaction. Instead, they're all reaching for a second piece.

I figure it's just some kind of anomalous reaction to not having tasted Breather in a year, and so I swallow what's in my mouth. The moment it goes down, I get a sharp pain in my head and flashes of zombie films play across my vision in bright, unforgiving color. Corpses tearing into humans and devouring flesh. Flaps of skin hanging out from between teeth and lips. Blood squirting out and dribbling down chins. Arms and legs torn from torsos and intestines eviscerated from body cavities.

And I realize I'm going to be sick.

In a panic, I look around for the nearest window and see the plastic bucket in the corner. I barely make it before the contents of my stomach come back up, including the Hot Pocket and the pesto tortellini.

Movie clips continue to play in my head and I'm putting two and two together, thinking this is related to the recent experiments administered by Bob. I'm also thinking that this isn't one of the Top Ten Moments in Zombie History. And that I might have just lowered the bar for zombies everywhere.

When it feels like I'm finally done, I wipe my mouth and look up to see everyone else staring at me. No one is chewing or making sounds of ecstatic pleasure, but instead they are all looking at me as if I'm some kind of circus freak.

"Are you okay?" asks Cameron.

"I'm fine," I say, and then vomit again into the bucket.

NINETEEN

"**W**hat was that all about?" asks Jeff, once the vomiting stops and I'm no longer curled up in a fetal position.

"I'm not sure," I say. "But I think it has something to do with these tests they were doing on me. Does anyone have a breath mint?"

"What tests?" asks Mykle.

I explain about the injections and the movie clips and the machine they hooked me up to at the research facility. I'm not a big Anthony Burgess or Stanley Kubrick fan, but I'm guessing Bob was conducting some kind of aversion therapy on me, in *A Zombie Clockwork Orange* kind of way.

"So are you saying you can't eat Breather?" says Jeff.

I think about how I was able to eat tortellini and chocolate chip cookies and drink hot chocolate without any problems and how the thought of eating Breather right now makes me want to gag.

"It kind of looks that way," I say.

"Well, that sucks," says Mykle, biting into a piece of Breather jerky.

"Does that mean the rescue plan is off?" says Cameron.

"No," I say, getting to my feet, attempting to regain some of the dignity of leadership that I lost while dry heaving into a piss bucket.

"What's the plan?" says Jeff.

"I'm still working on it."

So much for leadership.

Everyone's silent for several minutes as we try to come up with some brilliant plan to rescue nearly two dozen zombies.

"What about PETZ?" asks Cameron. "Can they help?"

"Maybe," I say. "But I don't know how to get hold of them. Anyone have a computer or a cell phone?"

The three of them shake their heads while Zack and Luke shrug. One of the problems about being a zombie is a lack of access to technology. No one's offering a calling plan or Internet service to a reanimated corpse.

"Okay," says Jeff. "Then it's just the six of us. So how do we get inside that place looking like this?"

I look around the room at my team of insurgents—dressed in hoodies, a Red Sox cap, and green tights and turtlenecks—and I wonder the same thing. We're like the zombie Village People.

Mykle is looking around at everyone, too, and when his gaze lands on me his face lights up. "Hey! What if we all dressed up like Santa Claus?"

I look down at myself as Zack and Luke start humming "Here Comes Santa Claus."

"Wouldn't we look suspicious?" asks Cameron. "Half a dozen Santas just walking around a research facility?"

"Not if we were there passing out candy canes or singing Christmas carols or something like that," says Mykle. "You know, spreading holiday cheer."

Everyone looks at me, so apparently I still have some sort of cachet in the leadership department.

"I like it," I say.

Why not? Especially since we don't have any other ideas.

"You really think that'll work?" asks Jeff.

I nod. "It's the best shot we have. Once we get inside I have a pretty good idea of the layout of the building and can find my way to the kennel. The biggest problem I can see is getting from here to there. A group of Santas walking through downtown Portland is bound to draw attention."

"What if we do it during SantaCon," says Mykle.

"What's SantaCon?" I say.

"It's an annual event that takes place every Christmas in a bunch of different cities," says Cameron. "People dress up in Santa costumes and allegedly go around the city spreading holiday cheer when really it's just a bunch of idiots getting drunk in a mass pub crawl."

"I've done it a couple of times," says Mykle. "There are, like, hundreds of Santas walking around all over Portland. It would be perfect."

"Okay," I say. "That sounds like it could work. Now

all we need to do is figure out how we're going to get the other zombies out without making a scene. It might help if we can recruit a couple more zombies to beef up our numbers. How much time do we have before Santa-Con?"

"It's today," says Mykle.

Well, that sort of pushes up the time table.

"Today?" says Cameron. "That doesn't give us enough time to prepare. And where are we supposed to get five more Santa suits?"

"Why do you always have to be so negative?" says Mykle.

"I'm not being negative," says Cameron. "I'm just stating the facts."

"I think the facts are that you're being a big negative douche bag," says Mykle.

Cameron folds his arms. "Well, excuse me if coming back from the dead and slowly decomposing in a basement hasn't provided me with a particularly rosy outlook."

"I bet you were a big negative douche bag before you reanimated," says Mykle.

"I'm not a douche bag."

"Yes, you are," says Mykle. "A total douche."

"Your immature attitude isn't constructive," says Cameron.

"Douche."

"Hey! If you two douche bags are done," says Jeff, "it just so happens that, hello? My sister owns a dry cleaners."

I love it when a plan comes together.

"I saw a bunch of Santa suits on the racks when I was up there a few nights ago," says Jeff. "I don't know how many, but I'm pretty sure there were at least five or six."

Mykle looks at Cameron and mouths the word *douche.* Cameron responds by rubbing his right eyebrow with his middle finger.

"Won't that cause problems with your sister?" I say.

"Probably," says Jeff. "But like you said, eventually you don't have anyone you can count on but yourself. Right?"

I nod, though I wonder if Jeff's attitude is based on my inspirational speech or how he feels now that he's eaten Breather. Even if it was dried and cured and looked like it came out of a sealed bag from a 7-Eleven aisle, once you've consumed human flesh, relationships with the living become a little more difficult.

"Are you sure we have enough time to pull everything together?" asks Jeff.

"I don't know," I say. "But I think this is probably our best chance, so it doesn't look like we have much of a choice."

We decide it's safer to use Zack and Luke's hideout as our staging point rather than the dry cleaners basement, so Jeff takes off to get the Santa suits with Cameron and Mykle, who are still arguing about being immature zombies and negative douche bags.

I stay behind with the twins, who curl up together on the floor to take a nap. I decide that looks like a good idea, too, so I lie down on the blanket next to them and close my eyes, trying not to think about the thick, heavy feeling that's continuing to take hold of me. Or how the very thought of eating Breather makes me want to throw up again.

Not long after I close my eyes, I feel Zack and Luke curled up on either side of me, like a couple of cats seeking warmth. The two of them next to me like this reminds me of Annie snuggling with me on the couch and I fall asleep with her on my mind.

IT'S CHRISTMAS MORNING. There's a tree decorated with lights and ornaments. Bright packages wrapped in ribbons and bows crowd around it. An empty stocking hangs by the fireplace. The name on the stocking says ANNIE. On a small table near the fireplace sits a plate of cookie crumbs and an empty glass that once contained milk.

In the background, Elvis Presley sings "Here Comes Santa Claus."

I sit on the couch in my Santa suit, drinking hot chocolate from a mug that says OHSU ALUMNUS. On the floor in front of the Christmas tree, Annie sorts through the presents dressed in her pink flannel pajamas with black and white cartoon bunnies. She picks up a package more than half the size of her, wrapped in gold paper, and turns to me.

"What is it?" she asks.

"I don't know," I say with a wink. "Why don't you open it?"

As Annie starts unwrapping her present, I notice a wet spot on the front of my jacket. When I investigate, I discover that my feeding tube is leaking a greenish fluid and that the flesh around it has started to turn black and become distended. The smell of decay drifts up and nearly causes me to gag.

Annie lets out a shriek. I look up, expecting her to be staring at me and screaming. Instead, she's holding a big stuffed panda bear and wearing a smile that brightens her entire face.

"Thank you, Santa!" she says, hugging the panda bear. "This is the best Christmas ever!"

I WAKE TO the sound of Jeff returning with Mykle and Cameron, each of them carrying a dry-cleaning bag containing a Santa Claus suit. Zack and Luke are already awake and humming "Here Comes Santa Claus."

"There were only three left," says Jeff. "I guess the rest got picked up already."

"What are we going to do now?" says Cameron.

I look at the three of them holding their Santa suits, then I look at Zack and Luke in their dark green tights and turtlenecks, looking at me and humming, and I get an idea.

"I think we can still make this work," I say. "But we're going to need fake beards for the three of you and hats for Zack and Luke. Maybe a few boxes of candy canes to hand out. Does anyone have any money?"

Cameron, Jeff, and Mykle all shake their heads as Luke jumps up and disappears through the door again. He comes back a minute later with a pillowcase that he hands to me. When I look inside, I see a bunch of loose change and what appears to be more than a couple hundred dollars in cash.

I'd ask them where they got the money, but they'd probably just answer with a smile or some cryptic phrase. And I really don't care. Plus this gives me an idea as to how I can help make someone's Christmas a little merrier.

"So what time does SantaCon get started?" I ask.

"Pretty early," says Mykle. "By nine or ten o'clock there's usually a bunch of Santas cruising around downtown. By noon, it's packed."

"Okay," I say. "We'll wait until after eleven to head out and get what we need, which leaves us plenty of time to figure out our plan."

Jeff walks up to me and says under his breath, "Are the six of us enough?"

"We'll be fine," I say. "After all, there were only seven of us when we stormed Sigma Chi."

"Yeah," says Jeff. "And look how good that turned out."

"I don't know about this," says Cameron, trying on his Santa pants, which are too short for him. "I think someone's going to be able to tell we're not Breathers."

"Don't be such a Negative Nancy," says Mykle, slipping into his jacket, his hat already perched atop his head. "There are going to be Santas everywhere. Who's going to suspect that any of them are zombies?"

TWENTY

"How many are there?" asks Duncan, standing on the corner of Couch and Eighth streets beneath the cloud-covered sun, an array of Santa Clauses reflected in his mirrored sunglasses.

"A lot more than I expected," says Shannon, turning to look at the three dozen or so men and women in various Santa Claus costumes walking up and down the street. She and Duncan have been searching the city streets since sunrise for a Santa Claus suit–clad Andy Warner, and after more than three hours, the number of Santas in downtown Portland has grown exponentially.

"How the hell are we supposed to find him in all of this?" says Duncan as they start walking again.

"I don't know. But we don't have much of a choice."

"Sure we do. We always have a choice. It's called free will. Unless you're a hard determinist like Martin Luther."

"Funny," says Shannon. "I never took you for the philosophical type."

"Hey, I'm a multifaceted guy," says Duncan. "Philosopher. Zombie handler. Ladies' man."

Shannon looks Duncan up and down. For some reason, she has a hard time believing he has much luck with the ladies.

"One time in college," he says, "I even took a class on philosophical zombies with a bunch of women."

"Congratulations."

"Hey, I take pride in my ability to multitask."

They walk past the Pearl Bakery at the corner of Couch and Ninth, where a mother and father try to comfort their young son, who is freaked out about all of the Santas.

"So how old were you when you found out there was no such thing as Santa Claus?" asks Duncan.

"I don't remember," says Shannon.

"Come on. Every kid remembers when their Santa cherry got popped."

"I don't know," says Shannon. "Nine or ten, I guess."

"I was eight," says Duncan. "My older sister told me just two weeks before the big guy was supposed to come. Completely fucked my Christmas."

They continue for a couple of blocks until they reach the corner of Couch and Eleventh, where a Santa in an ill-fitting suit sits on the sidewalk out in front of Powell's Books with a sign that says:

HO HO HO, HOW ABOUT SOME DOUGH?
(BEER AND WINE ACCEPTED)

"Ho ho ho," says Santa, from beneath his dirty hat and above his fake beard as he holds out his donation cup. "Merry Christmas."

"I'm Jewish," says Duncan, then he reaches down and yanks off the fake beard, revealing someone who isn't Andy Warner.

"Hey, man!" says the Santa, replacing his beard. "That's not cool!"

"Neither is using the iconic image of the Christmas spirit to guilt people into giving you their hard-earned money," says Duncan. He turns to Shannon. "Bupkes."

"Then we keep looking."

"Hey," says Santa, holding out his donation cup as Shannon and Duncan start to walk away. "How about some holiday spirits for old St. Nick?"

"Don't you mean *spirit*?" says Duncan.

"Last I checked," says Santa, "they don't sell spirit at the liquor store."

"I like a homeless Santa with honesty," says Duncan, who pulls out a dollar and puts it in the donation cup.

Santa looks into the cup. "Any chance you could like me a little more?"

Shannon and Duncan spend another ten minutes walking up and down the streets in the Pearl District, stopping to check out every drunken Santa they pass who might be their zombie, but the only zombies they find are in plastic to-go cups.

"This is pointless," says Duncan as a trio of drunken Santas walk past singing a botched rendition of "We Three Kings" before one of them throws up in the gutter. "How much longer are we going to keep looking for him?"

"As long as it takes," says Shannon.

"Ballpark figure?"

"As long as it takes."

"Can we stop and get something to eat?"

"Later."

"How much later?" he says. "It's almost noon. I'm starving."

"If you want to tell Carter you stopped to grab some lunch while our prize zombie was on the loose in downtown Portland, be my guest."

That shuts him up, but not for long.

"How about a quick snack?" he says. "I'll just run into a store and grab a banana and a doughnut and a Frappuccino. I'll be in and out, lickety-split."

Shannon looks at Duncan and sees her face reflected back in his sunglasses, stretched wide like she's looking into a couple of miniature funhouse mirrors.

"Come on," he says. "You can wait outside and keep an eye out for Santa-It. I'll only be a couple of minutes. Please?"

"Fine," she says. "There's a Rite Aid a couple of blocks away. But make it fast."

TWENTY-ONE

"Did you find everything you needed?" the cashier asks as he rings up my purchase, which consists of five packs of candy canes, four boxes of ornaments, three fake Santa beards, two strings of Christmas lights, and a single stocking two feet long.

I also got a drawstring laundry bag, a bunch of stocking stuffers, and a three-pack of boxers. Hey, even zombies need clean underwear.

"Yes, thank you," I say, looking the cashier in the eye and smiling. It's exhilarating to be out during the day in public, mingling among the living without their knowledge, surrounded by Breathers who accept you as one of them, but knowing that at any moment you might be found out.

"Oh, and those, too," I say, indicating the new Santa hats worn by Zack and Luke, who are standing on either side of me. They flash the cashier matching smiles, then walk over to a display of scarves and knit hats and start petting them.

"What's up with those two?" asks the cashier.

"They're my elves," I say. "Every Santa needs his elves."

The cashier glances at them. "They're kind of creepy."

"Yeah, I get that a lot."

As I watch the cashier bag up the decorations and candy canes and fake beards, I find myself falling into old habits. I used to size up Breathers whenever I saw them, trying to determine what kind of dishes they resembled. What they inspired in my inner Bobby Flay. Some of them looked like stews, some looked like stir-fries, and some looked more like Stroganoffs. But every one caused me to salivate at the culinary possibilities.

That was before the research facility. Before the aversion therapy. Before I was turned into an undead Alex DeLarge.

But even though the thought of eating the cashier makes me feel a little nauseous, he definitely looks like lasagna.

"Will that be cash or card?" says the cashier.

"Cash," I say, and hand him some of Zack and Luke's money. He hands me back my change and my bags and wishes me a merry Christmas.

I collect the twins and head toward the exit. On the way out, I bump into a short guy wearing mirrored sunglasses who snaps at me to "sober up and watch where the hell I'm going" before he continues into the store.

I turn and watch him go and decide that he looks like rump roast.

Zack and Luke start to go after him, but I hold up a finger and shake my head. "No."

The three of us walk out of the store and turn up the street to go meet the others when I glimpse a bald woman standing on the sidewalk next to a parking meter less than ten feet away. She's looking down the street so I only see her profile, but I know her face. I've seen it countless times from multiple angles and I would recognize her anywhere.

I look around to see if the guy with the 1970s porn star mustache is here, too, but I don't see any sign of him. When I look back at the bald woman, she's staring right at me.

Well, this is awkward.

People often speak of time standing still. Moments when everything else around them ceases to move or exist and they have absolute clarity and focus on an object or a situation. Like when they meet their true love or make a game-winning play or survive a life-threatening experience.

I've never had one of those moments until now. Not that I can remember. And although the moment seems to stretch out for minutes, in reality it lasts only a few seconds. But that's enough time for me to realize that running would be pointless. I don't have the mobility or the stamina. Plus I don't want to cause a scene.

There's really only one thing I can do.

"Stay," I say, handing my bags to Zack and Luke. Then I walk toward the bald woman, taking slow, measured steps, maintaining eye contact until I'm standing directly in front of her.

She hasn't moved or called out for help or alerted anyone to my presence, but I know she probably has a cell phone and a stun baton on her and that it's only a matter of seconds before she uses one or the other. I just hope there's some sense of compassion somewhere inside of her; otherwise I'm just wasting my breath.

I'm trying to think of the best way to appeal to her but I know I don't have much time, so I decide to keep it simple.

"Please," I say.

She continues to look at me, her eyes never leaving mine. Then her gaze flicks away over my shoulder for a moment as her right hand reaches inside her jacket and I expect to feel the shock of a stun baton at any moment.

Instead she removes something else, something I can't see. Then she reaches out and takes my right hand with her left and places the contents of her right hand into mine. When I look down at my palm, I see a plastic syringe filled with a brown liquid.

"Go," she says, then she turns and takes a couple of steps and looks the other way.

I don't try to thank her or attempt to verify what's in the syringe, but I close my hand around it and turn in the opposite direction and walk over to Zack and Luke, whose perpetual smiles have been replaced with concerned expressions that shift from me to the bald woman.

I realize that I don't even know her name.

"It's okay," I say, slipping the syringe into my pocket. "Let's go."

As we walk away up the sidewalk, I glance back and see the rump roast emerge from the store with a sandwich in one hand and a Frappuccino in the other. He approaches the bald woman, who never once looks my way. Then they're lost behind a sea of Santas and Santaettes singing "Rudolph the Red-Nosed Reindeer."

TWENTY-TWO

Cameron is standing alone at the corner of Thirteenth and Washington, looking like an abandoned dog waiting for his master. Either that or an angry mother waiting for her children.

"Where are Jeff and Mykle?" I say, handing Cameron his beard.

"In there." He points across the street to a bar called Scooter's.

"What the hell are they doing in there?" I say, as I transfer the rest of the stuff I bought into the drawstring laundry bag.

"Shots, I think." Cameron slips the elastic around his ears. "I told them it was a bad idea, but they wouldn't listen to me."

Big surprise.

I hand the laundry bag to Cameron. "I'll get them. You three stay here."

Cameron looks inside the bag. "Hey, what's all this stuff for?"

"I'll explain later," I say and head across the street.

I'm still a little unsettled from my encounter with the bald woman. Compassion from a Breather isn't something I have a lot of experience with, so I don't know whether to trust her. The fact that she knows I'm dressed like Santa and was downtown apparently looking for me means she's probably not the only one who knows, which should put the kibosh on our rescue plan. But at this point, we don't have much choice.

Inside Scooter's are close to two dozen Santas, along with a handful of regular customers who appear either amused or annoyed with the excess drunken holiday cheer—more than enough Breathers to cause a problem should any one of them realize that two of the customers are zombies. Three, if you include me. But I'm hoping I can get Jeff and Mykle out of here without any unnecessary attention.

"Hey Andy!" Mykle waves to me from the far end of bar. "Get over here!"

So much for keeping a low profile.

Mykle and Jeff are at the bar with half a dozen other Santas, half-finished beers in their hands and Jell-O shots in front of them. Neither Jeff nor Mykle is wearing a fake beard because I hadn't bought them yet, which means everyone can see the claw marks on Mykle's face and Jeff's festering piercings.

I don't know what they were thinking, but I need to get them the hell out of here before someone calls Animal Control.

When I walk up, everyone cheers and Jeff puts a beer

in my hand while one of the Breather Santas hands me a Jell-O shot.

"You're just in time!" shouts another Santa, raising his own Jell-O shot in the air. "Ho ho Jell-O!"

Everyone raises their shots and responds in kind, then sucks down their shots. I don't want to look like a party pooper, so I do the same.

"Dude, you were right," says one of the Breather Santas, pointing at me. "He totally looks like Santa. Nice!"

He puts his right hand up in the air. The last thing I want to do is start making friends, but it's bad form to leave him hanging. So we high-five.

I look over at Jeff and give him a wide-eyed *what-the-fuck-are-you-thinking-we-have-to-get-out-of-here* look. But before Jeff can explain, one of the other Santas puts an arm around me and points at Mykle with his beer. "This dude's got the best idea here. Mauled-By-A-Bear Santa. Fucking. Genius."

I look at Mykle, who orders up another round of PBRs and throws one of Zack and Luke's twenties on the bar, which helps to explain why he and Jeff are so popular. Still, we can't stay here and party, so I pull Jeff aside for a little one-on-one.

"What the fuck are you two doing?" I say. "We need to go."

"I know," he says. "But Mykle and I thought it might be a good idea if we had a few additional bodies to help get your friends out."

I look at the handful of drunken Santas saying "dude" and high-fiving each other, and I can't help but think that Jerry would love it here. "How do you figure they can help?"

"Once we get inside, we pull a bait and switch," Jeff says with a smile. "Six human and six zombie Santas go in, but twelve zombie Santas come out."

I look back at the group of Breathers laughing and drinking around Mykle, who smiles and raises his beer as one of the Santa Breathers gives him a high-five.

Maybe they've got something here.

"Okay," I say. "You've got two minutes. Get however many of your friends are going with us and let's go."

"Where are you going?" Jeff asks as I head toward the back of the bar.

"To the bathroom."

Once in the bathroom, I lock the door, then I sit down on top of the toilet and remove the syringe from my pocket. I pull up my coat and insert the syringe into my chopped-off feeding tube. I don't have any time to second-guess myself or to question the motives of the bald woman. I just have to hope this is what I think it is. And that it works. At this point, what have I got to lose?

My fingers feel stiff and clumsy around the syringe and I'm afraid I'm going to drop it or miss and the contents are going to spill out onto the floor. Then my thumb is pressing down on the plunger and the brown liquid is flowing into my stomach.

The reaction is almost immediate. While I still feel heavy and sluggish, I sense something different going on inside me, a kind of awakening. Like the electricity had been turned off and someone just flipped a switch and things are starting to hum again. I don't know how long the electricity will stay on, but I hope it's long enough.

Two minutes later I'm standing out across the street from Scooter's with Mykle, Jeff, Cameron, Zack, Luke, and four Breather Santas who have been bribed with the promise of free drinks. Mykle and Jeff have donned their Santa beards while Zack and Luke eye the four Breathers. I wonder if this is a good idea or if all we've done is provide some snacks to take along on our expedition. Which is going to include a couple of pit stops, though I haven't mentioned that yet to anyone.

The electricity inside me is humming, the lights coming on one by one. Even my legs feel stronger than before. Maybe it's just my imagination, but I feel like a new zombie.

"Everyone ready?" I say.

My band of Santas confirms its readiness with a hearty round of *Ho ho hos.* Zack and Luke just jump up and down and applaud.

"All right," I say, hoisting my sack of goodies over my shoulder. "Let's get our merry on."

TWENTY-THREE

Annie sits alone at the kitchen table picking at her lunch, which consists of a half-eaten peanut butter and jelly sandwich, a glass of milk, and some potato chips. She picks up her sandwich and takes an unenthusiastic bite, then puts it back down. She knows she should be hungry since she didn't really eat any breakfast but she just doesn't seem to have an appetite.

Her mother is still asleep.

Annie knows better than to try to wake her up, but there was the promise that they'd go get a Christmas tree today. She hopes her mother wakes up soon because it's already two o'clock and Christmas is only three days away.

But Annie knows her mother is better at breaking her promises than she is at keeping them.

The television keeps her company in the background, *The Santa Clause* playing on TBS. She glances over at the TV and wishes Santa was here to watch it with her.

Yesterday was the best day Annie has had in a long time, ever since her father died. Having Santa here with her was almost like having her father back and it made her remember how much she missed him and how much more fun Christmas was with her father here. She knows Santa probably can't give her what she really wants for Christmas, but part of her still wishes it will come true.

Annie finally gives up on her lunch and takes her dishes to the sink, her hopes of getting a Christmas tree fading along with her appetite. Against her better judgment, she walks down the hallway and knocks on her mother's bedroom door. When she doesn't hear anything, Annie puts her ear to the door and listens, then sighs and goes to use the bathroom.

While she's washing her hands, she thinks she hears someone knock on the bathroom door. "Mom?" she calls out. But there's no answer.

When Annie walks out of the bathroom, her mother's bedroom door is still closed. She's about to knock on it again when she hears voices outside on the street, people laughing and some of them singing. She thinks maybe they're Christmas carolers, except there have never been Christmas carolers in her neighborhood before.

Someone knocks on the front door.

Annie walks down the hallway to the front window and looks out through the venetian blinds to see what's going on and lets out a gasp.

There are a bunch of Santas standing on the front porch and on the stairs and on the sidewalk. There are even a couple of elves. And they're carrying a Christmas tree!

Annie runs over to the front door and opens it wide,

a big smile spreading across her face. Standing in front of everyone else with a bag over his shoulder is Santa Claus.

"Merry Christmas, Annie!" he calls out.

Annie gives Santa a big hug as some of the others start singing "We Wish You a Merry Christmas" and they all come inside. First Santa, then the elves, then all the helpers. The ones carrying the tree smell bad, like they haven't taken a bath in a while and fell asleep in some garbage, but she doesn't mind. The apartment is full of Santas and elves and Christmas, and right now, that's all that matters.

"Why don't you put the tree up over there," says Santa, pointing to the corner by the front window and setting down his bag.

Three of the fake Santas clear a space and set up the tree while the others go into the kitchen and start rummaging around in the cabinets. Annie doesn't know what they're looking for, but when they find her mother's bottles above the refrigerator, they let out a cheer.

"Dude!" says one of them. "Who wants tequila?"

Annie gives the real Santa another big hug. "I missed you, Santa. I'm glad you came back."

"Me too," he says. "I brought something for your tree."

Santa opens his bag and reaches inside and pulls out some Christmas lights, a box of candy canes, and several boxes of ornaments.

"Yay!" Annie says, and claps. "Thank you so much, Santa!"

"Zack. Luke," says Santa. The two elves appear at his side like magic and Annie realizes with delight that they're twins. Santa hands them the decorations, which they take without a word over to the tree and get to work.

"Are they real?" she asks, pointing at the elves. She knows it's not polite to point, but she can't help herself.

Santa looks at them for a few moments before answering. "Yes. They're most definitely real."

"Awesome," says Annie. "I've never seen a real elf before."

The elf twins start putting the lights up on the tree as the three fake Santas remove the ornaments from the boxes. One of them is taller with glasses while another one talks with a funny accent that reminds Annie of a cartoon character.

"Why are the elves so tall?" she asks. "I thought elves were short. And how come they don't have pointed ears?"

"They're special elves," says Santa. "They're not like the ones you're used to seeing."

The elves look over at Annie and give her matching smiles.

"They're cute," she says. "Do you think they'd like some Gummi Bears?"

"Well, I don't think that's what they're in the mood for just now," says Santa.

"What are they in the mood for?" she asks.

Santa hesitates before answering. "Something else."

In the kitchen, two of the fake Santas are doing shots of tequila and high-fiving each other while the other two look through the cabinets and refrigerator.

"I can't find any margarita mix," says one of them.

"Just use orange juice, dude," says another.

Annie turns and looks at the Christmas tree, which already has a bunch of candy canes and two dozen shiny red and gold ornaments hanging from its branches. She hasn't had a Christmas tree in three years and she thinks this is the most perfect one she's ever seen. A moment later, one of the elf twins plugs in the lights and the tree lights up in reds and blues and greens. Annie applauds again. Then the elves start humming "Deck the Halls" and pretty soon everyone starts singing as the fake Santas in the kitchen walk around the room passing out drinks to everyone.

"I have something else for you," says the real Santa, who reaches into his bag again and pulls out a big red stocking and hands it to Annie. "I wasn't able to find a big panda bear on short notice, but I thought you might like one of these."

Annie takes the stocking from him and holds it against her chest. It doesn't have her name on it but it doesn't matter. She loves it. She gives Santa another big hug along with a kiss on the cheek.

"So where should we hang it?" says Santa.

Annie looks around and points at the wall next to the heater. "How about there?"

She grabs a hammer and a nail from a drawer in the kitchen, then leads Santa over to the heater, where he pounds the nail into the wall and hangs the stocking as the other fake Santas continue to sing and drink and the elf twins curl up next to each other on the couch. Then Santa reaches into his bag and pulls out a bunch of toys and candy that he stuffs into the stocking.

Annie looks around at everyone and everything and laughs.

This is the best, most awesome Christmas *ever.*

"Annie, what is all this *noise*?!"

Annie stops laughing and turns to find her mother standing at the entrance of the hallway in a nightshirt and underwear, rubbing her eyes with one hand while she steadies herself on the wall with the other. Then her mother looks around and seems to see everyone for the first time.

Santa and the fake Santas and the elf twins just stare back, no one moving or singing or saying a word. Then one of the fake Santas lets out a snort of laughter and the elves start to giggle and all of the other Santas shout out, "Merry Christmas!"

"What are you all doing here?" says her mother, her speech slightly slurred.

"They're my friends," says Annie.

"Well, your friends need to keep it down," she says. "I'm trying to sleep."

Then her mother turns around and staggers back down the hallway, closing her bedroom door behind her.

"Whoa. Dude," says one of the fake Santas. "She was hot."

"Total MILF," says one of the others.

And then they high-five each other.

"Okay, ladies," says the fake Santa with the funny accent. "Time to clear out."

Santa Claus kneels down in front of Annie. "I'm sorry, but we have to go."

"But I don't want you to," she says, hugging him. "I'm having so much fun."

"I am, too." He hugs her back. "But we have some other people we have to visit and other Christmases we need to make merry."

"I know," she says, but doesn't let go. She just wants to hold on to him and have him stay with her. "I wish you could stay with me forever."

He doesn't respond, but he hugs her tighter and that means more than anything he could say.

Finally she lets go and Santa stands up. Most everyone else has already gone out the front door and she can hear them laughing and singing outside. The only other ones remaining are the elf twins, who give her a smile and then take off their caps at the same time before bowing together. Then they slip out the front door and stand waiting on the porch.

"Will you come back to visit me?" asks Annie.

"I hope so," says Santa. "But if I don't, I want you to know that I'll always be watching."

"Promise?" she says, as her eyes well up with tears.

"I promise."

"Cross your heart?"

He crosses his heart. "You bet."

"I won't say the last part," she says.

He nods at her and smiles. "Good-bye, Annie."

"Good-bye, Santa," she says, and watches him walk to the front door through her tears.

Santa stops and looks back at her with a smile, then he puts a finger aside of his nose, gives her a wink, and out the door he goes.

TWENTY-FOUR

"So who was that little girl?" asks Jeff as we walk away from Annie's.

"Someone I made a promise to," I say.

"What kind of a promise?" says Mykle.

"Just trying to help her have a happy Christmas," I say.

Though as much as I enjoyed seeing the smile on Annie's face and hearing her laugher, I still haven't given her what she really wants for Christmas. But how the hell am I supposed to get her mother to spend more time with her?

The ten of us continue in silence. Rather, six of us are silent while the four Breather Santas are singing an off-color version of "Jingle Bells."

"So do you think this is really going to work?" says Cameron.

Our plan is to gain entrance into the research facility, get a kennel key from one of the interns or lab techs, free the other zombies, disguise Patrick and several others with the Santa suits from the four drunken Breathers, then escape in the chaos and confusion.

Piece of cake.

To be honest, I don't know if we can even get into the research facility. Or get a key to the kennel cages. Or get out of there without getting caught. But someone has to believe it'll work, so it might as well be me.

"Yes," I say. "I do."

"What happens if somebody recognizes you?" says Cameron. "What are we going to do then?"

"We'll worry about that if it happens," I say. "But right now, I'd be more concerned about our friends."

Up ahead of us, the four Santa Breathers have all stopped at a neighboring house decorated with religious Christmas motifs and are in the process of taking a leak on a nativity scene.

AS IT TURNS out, all of the exterior entrances directly into the research facility wing of the OHSU campus are locked and require an ID badge to enter, which means the only way for us to gain access is through the hospital.

"Is this going to be a problem?" says Jeff.

"We're fine," I say. "It'll be like paying to see a movie at the cineplex and then sneaking into the second movie for free."

"I always got caught when I did that," says Cameron.

"Douche," says Mykle.

While getting into the OHSU campus proves to be as easy as catching a cold, finding our way to the research facility entrance turns out to be more like trying to catch a cab on New Year's Eve. It doesn't help when you have a handful of drunken Breathers who keep getting distracted by shiny things and vending machines and cute nurses.

"Oh dude, check *her* out."

"I think someone needs to take her temperature because she is on *fire*."

And the requisite high-five.

Fortunately, most of the staff is tolerant of our presence when we openly demonstrate that we're here to spread Christmas cheer to the patients. It helps that Zack and Luke perform synchronized mime routines that enchant everyone.

They really need to have their own reality show.

With all of the spreading of yuletide joy, it takes us more than an hour to make it through the hospital. Eventually, after handing out a bunch of candy canes and belting out some mangled Christmas carols and herding the Breathers away from the nurses and the zombies away from the Breathers, we reach the interior entrance to the research facility. The good news is, our four drunken Santas have either sobered up or hit a wall and have grown somewhat more subdued. The bad news is, there are two security guards standing in front of the double doors and we aren't authorized to enter.

"Well, what do we have here?" says the first security guard, with a faint Boston accent and an ID badge that says W. Banks.

"It looks like a band of misfit Santas," says the other one, whose badge identifies him as J. Ramirez.

Zack and Luke immediately go into their traveling

minstrel routine, which gets a laugh and some polite applause out of Banks.

"Nice," he says. "You two are a couple of regular circus elves."

"What's your business here?" says Ramirez, who isn't as impressed.

"We're just spreading some holiday cheer," I say, handing each of them a candy cane. "We've been going around the hospital and some of the staff sent us this way."

"Well, this is as far as you get," says Ramirez. "No one gets through without a valid ID badge or visitor's pass."

I figured this might happen, but I was hoping we'd be able to charm our way past security. If it turns out we can't, then we'll have to go to Plan B, which doesn't involve quite so much charm.

"Come on, Ramirez," says Banks, sucking on his candy cane. "It's Christmas. Lighten up, for Christ's sake."

"After what happened yesterday?" says Ramirez.

"What happened yesterday?" asks Jeff, laying on a slightly thicker Boston accent than normal.

"Just a little security problem," says Banks. "You from Boston?"

"Southie," says Jeff. "Moved here two years ago."

"No shit?" says Banks. "Me too. Only I moved here nearly ten years ago. My brothers moved to Charlestown, but my mom and dad are still in Southie. You got any brothers?"

"Two sisters," says Jeff. "Both of 'em here in Portland."

"Nice," says Banks. "It's good to have family around, you know? They stick by you through thick and thin."

"That they do," says Jeff, without a trace of irony.

No one else says anything. It's as though we can all sense the Boston camaraderie building and no one wants to break the momentum. Most of us, anyway.

"Red Sox!" shouts one of the Santa Breathers, then he puts up his hand for a high-five, but his drinking buddies are all in standing comas.

"Don't mind him," says Jeff. "He's just a douche bag."

Banks looks us all over. "You think you can you keep him under control?"

"Absolutely," says Jeff.

Banks nods, then stands aside and opens up one of the double doors.

"What the hell are you doing?" says Ramirez.

"Look at them," says Banks. "They don't look like they're here to cause any trouble. Are you guys here to cause trouble?"

Everyone shakes their heads.

"See?" says Banks.

Some Breathers are so trusting. Taking food from strangers. Providing personal information to a voice over the phone. Letting a bunch of zombies dressed up like Santa into a restricted area of a research facility.

"I don't think this is a good idea," says Ramirez.

"I'll chaperone them if it'll make you feel better," says Banks as we start to file through the doorway. "They're just here to sing some songs and pass out candy canes. What's the worst that could happen?"

TWENTY-FIVE

We're walking along a hallway past examination rooms and labs. So far we've only come across a handful of people to serenade and gift with candy canes, as most of the rooms have either been empty or locked. Apparently Saturdays are slow days for experimenting on reanimated corpses. Either that or everyone is out looking for me.

About a hundred feet ahead of us, I can see that the hallway comes to an end and forms a T with another hallway, which, unless I'm completely turned around, leads to the kennel. So far the only keys I've seen are hanging from the belt of our chaperone, which makes things a little more complicated than I'd planned.

I'm trying to figure out how I'm going to get hold of those keys when one of the drunken Santas says, "Dude, I don't feel so good." I look back at him and notice that he's pale and he has a glazed, hollow expression. If I didn't know any better, I'd say he was a zombie.

"I think I'm gonna be sick," he says, then pushes open a door and disappears inside.

"Wait for me," says one of the other Santas. "I've gotta take a leak."

I had a feeling bringing along a bunch of Breathers was going to be a problem. Once they start drinking and break the seal, they have to stop to pee every ten minutes.

When the door closes, I notice that the sign on the front doesn't say MEN'S ROOM but OBSERVATION ROOM.

"Hey!" says Banks. "You can't go in there!"

"I'll get them," I say, then go through the door after them, hoping this doesn't completely screw our plans.

I walk up the short flight of steps and think about all the times I looked up and saw the bald woman and the mustached man in one of these observation rooms while I was suspended by cables or strapped to a cadaver board. It occurs to me that one or both of them could be at the top of these stairs right now, looking through the Plexiglas window at some other poor zombie soul getting shot or burned or dismembered.

When I reach the top of the stairs, the only ones in the observation room are the two Breather Santas. While the one who had to pee isn't taking a leak in the corner, the other Santa is throwing up on one of the chairs. When I see what's taking place in the examination room below, my own empty stomach twists around on itself.

Patrick is spread-eagled on an examination table, naked as usual, while Bob stands over him with an acetylene torch. A moment later, Bob starts cooking the flesh on Patrick's left leg.

"Dude," says the Santa who had to pee. "That's gnarly."

"Ah for Christ's sake," says Banks from behind me. "That's it. The fun's over. You all have to get out of here. Right now."

I turn around and see the security guard standing at the back row of seats with his hands on his belt, where he carries his gun and his stun baton and his set of keys. Just behind him at the top of the stairs appear Zack and Luke. Everyone else, I'm guessing, is still out in the hallway.

There are times when you realize you don't have any choice and that you have to abandon the plans you've made and accept the hand that you're dealt. When you realize that you have to accept defeat.

This is not one of those times.

"Zack. Luke," I say. "Plan B."

"What's Plan B?" says Banks.

I'm guessing he never expected those to be his last words, but sometimes life doesn't let you go out with a meaningful quote.

Before Banks can say anything else, Zack puts a hand over his mouth and Luke grabs the stun baton and zaps him into submission. While I'd like to cut Banks some slack for helping us to get inside, we can't risk him waking up and coming after us. Plus Zack and Luke have been good boys and I'm a firm believer in positive reinforcement. So I don't scold them when they bite into his throat and start eating him.

Behind me, the two Breathers start screaming.

Watching Zack and Luke eat the security guard gets my aversion therapy Pavlovian response going, with clips of zombie films flashing in my head. It's all I can do to keep from throwing up. So I grab the stun baton and the keys from the security guard's belt and try to think about Woody Allen films instead.

"When you're done . . . meet me down . . . there," I say to Zack and Luke, gagging and looking away from them and pointing toward the examination room before I run down the stairs, switching to Tyler Perry films, but that only makes me feel worse.

I throw open the door and stumble into the hallway, dry heaving.

"What happened?" says Mykle.

"Plan B," I say in between heaves.

"Plan B?" says Cameron. "What's Plan B?"

Apparently that's a popular catchphrase.

"Hey," says one of the other two Breathers. "Where are Matt and Brad?"

I'm guessing those are the two I left in the observation room with Zack and Luke.

"Busy," I say and hand the keys to Jeff. "The kennel is at the end of the hallway, all the way to the left. Start letting everyone out and I'll meet you there."

"Where are you going?" says Jeff.

I stand up and take a deep breath, then grip the stun baton. "To see an old friend," I say, and head toward the examination room.

TWENTY-SIX

Shannon sits in Carter's office, looking out the window at the body farm as the late afternoon sun fades behind the clouds moving in from the west. Behind her, Carter is on the phone talking to Recovery, but she's not paying attention to his conversation. All she can hear is the voice of Andy Warner and the single word he spoke to her.

Please.

When she'd seen him standing outside the Rite Aid, she'd been caught off guard. She hadn't expected that they would find him. Not just her and Duncan, but any of the Handler or Recovery teams. After twenty-four hours, she figured Andy Warner would have already gone into hiding or made his way out of town.

Why he was still around both perplexed and intrigued her. But more than anything, seeing him on the street, looking as human as everyone else and walking up to her and speaking that single, plaintive word made her completely doubt the purpose of what she was doing.

In spite of her interest in Andy Warner and the admiration she had for him, she never considered that she would act against her orders or contradict her training. She'd been a Handler for more than three years and had never experienced any conflict of interest.

But the moment he spoke to her, without thinking and before she knew what she was doing, she'd given him the syringe.

At the time she knew it was the right thing to do. Even as she and Duncan had walked around downtown Portland for another two hours and she'd pretended like nothing had happened, she felt good about what she'd done. But sitting here in Carter's office with the daylight waning and the clouds waxing, the weight of her decision settles over her, the consequences of what could happen if someone found out, and she wonders if, given the chance to do it over again, she'd make the same decision.

"How much do you think he gets paid for doing that?" asks Duncan.

Shannon turns to Duncan, who is eating Reese's Pieces out of a box he bought at Rite Aid while he watches one of the video monitors, on which is shown the examination room where Bob Rudolph performs most of his experiments. This time, it's Andy's neighbor, Patrick, who is the subject.

Patrick is strapped down with his arms and legs spread out like the Vitruvian Man by Leonardo da Vinci. Only instead of a blend of art and science, Patrick is a canvas for Bob's unique artistry. At the moment, Bob is just finishing up charring both of Patrick's legs with an acetylene torch, which he sets aside before picking up a bone saw.

Shannon looks away.

"I bet he makes twice what we do," says Duncan, eating Reese's Pieces like he's watching a movie. "Probably more. What do you think?"

"I think you have some serious detachment issues," says Shannon.

"What?" says Duncan, looking up at the monitor. "It's just a zombie."

Behind them, Carter slams the phone down. "Nothing. Not a goddamn thing. And a town full of fucking Santas. How the hell does something like this happen?"

Carter stands there a moment seething, then he grabs a ceramic coffee mug off his desk and hurls it against the wall.

This is the first time in the three years she's worked with Carter that Shannon has seen him upset. She used to think his perpetually calm demeanor was on the unsettling side, but seeing him lose control like this is worse.

"How do we know it's dressed like Santa?" says Carter. "Are the two of you sure it stole that Santa outfit? Maybe it was just teenagers. Maybe we're wasting our time looking for a fucking needle in a fucking haystack!"

Shannon sits there not saying a word, knowing better than to speak up. Duncan doesn't say anything, either, though he continues to eat his Reese's Pieces.

"I want you two to go back out to that house," says

Carter. "Right now. See what else you can find. Make sure you didn't miss something."

Shannon gets to her feet and Duncan follows her lead, but then he stops and points at the video monitor and says, "Maybe I'm wrong, but isn't that who we're looking for?"

They all watch as a Santa Claus enters the examination room, walks up behind Bob as he's preparing to saw off Patrick's left arm, and zaps him with a stun baton.

Duncan throws another handful of candy into his mouth. "I'm guessing we're not going to the house now."

Carter is on the phone. "Ramirez? What the hell is going on? There's a fucking Santa with a stun baton in my examination room!"

Shannon watches as Andy zaps Bob again before he starts unstrapping Patrick from the table and she realizes that he's come back to rescue the others. And with Recovery and all the other Handlers out looking for him, there's no one here to handle him.

No one except for her and Duncan.

TWENTY-SEVEN

I finish unstrapping Patrick's wrists and ankles and help him off the table. Although his legs are badly burned, it appears to be surface mutilation, leaving the muscles intact and functioning. Had I been another couple of minutes, Patrick would have been minus his left arm, which would have made it difficult for him to hug me.

Patrick wraps his arms around me and holds me tight. The fact that he's naked doesn't bother me as much as the feeling that we can't afford the luxury of a happy reunion.

"It's good to see you, too," I say and break the embrace. "But we have to go."

He points to Bob, who lies on the floor twitching. I wish I could do something poetically appropriate, but I don't have the time to electrocute him or pour acid on his genitals. I'd lean down and take a bite out of him for good measure, but I'd just throw him back up.

Being a zombie who can't eat human flesh is becoming an inconvenience.

Instead I zap Bob again with the stun baton, then Patrick and I lift him up and strap him down to the table. Before Patrick and I leave the examination room, I zap Bob once more for fun and Patrick grabs a pair of surgical shears from the instrument tray.

The hallway is eerily silent, with neither a footstep nor a scream to be heard. I look around for the twins but don't see any sign of them. And I don't have the time to wait.

Patrick and I hurry down to the end of the hallway, then stop and look around the corner to make sure the coast is clear. Like our own hallway, this one is deserted.

Either most of the staff is on holiday break or everyone's busy mutilating zombies.

When we reach the kennel, I look through the rectangular window in the door and see that Jeff and Cameron and Mykle are inside, having unlocked more than half of the cages. The other two Breather Santas are in there, too. Apparently they haven't figured out that SantaCon is over.

"Hey," says one of them when Patrick and I enter. "What happened to the free beer?"

"Yeah," says the other. "And why is that dude naked?"

"Because I'm allergic to cotton," says Patrick.

I look at Patrick and realize that he's removed his stitches with the surgical shears, which he passes around to the other zombies.

"So that's why you never wore one of the hospital gowns," I say.

"It makes me break out in a rash," says Patrick.

Although rashes don't tend to cause a lot of physical discomfort when you're a zombie, familiar routines don't die even when you do.

"Where are the twins?" asks Mykle.

"They're a little preoccupied," I say.

"Are Matt and Brad with them?" asks one of the Breathers.

"More or less."

Jeff has opened nearly all of the cages while half of the zombies have cut out their stitches and are heading out the door into the hallway, many of them thanking us as they leave. Hillary doesn't say anything, just kisses me on the cheek on her way out.

At this point the idea of any zombies getting out of here disguised as Santa Claus is pretty much toast, but at least they have the ability to fend for themselves a little more easily. Get a bite to eat. Maybe grab something to go.

"Dude," says one of the Breathers, looking around. "What's up with all these people with their mouths sewn shut?"

"I don't know," says the other one. "But it looks like this party is over. Come on. Let's go get something to eat."

As the two of them walk out of the kennel, I look up and see the camera mounted above the door and realize that in spite of the lack of resistance we've encountered, someone knows we're here. Which means we need to go.

"Oh Christ," says Jeff. "Jesus, no."

I turn to see Jeff unlocking the cage that holds Heather, the youngest and newest zombie. She's still shaking and terrified, her eyes wide and her arms trembling, but when Jeff opens the cage and steps inside and takes hold of Heather, her eyes close and I can see that she's sobbing. Then Jeff starts crying and the two of them collapse together on the floor of the cage.

It doesn't occur to me until now that Jeff's younger sister, the one who was in the car crash with him and ended up in a coma, is the same Heather.

I'm guessing she must have recently died or been taken off life support, but it's apparent Jeff had no idea what had happened to her. Or that she'd reanimated.

They remain in an embrace for a few moments, then Jeff stands up and helps his sister to her feet. But when he starts to lead her out of the cage, she grabs on to the bars and closes her eyes and starts shaking her head and whining.

"It's okay, Heather," says Jeff, still crying. "I'm here. I'll take care of you. I promise."

She just keeps shaking her head and making that high-pitched whine as she slides down to her knees, still holding on to the bars.

Out in the hallway, I hear the sound of voices. Feet running. Someone shouting. Then a single gunshot, followed by more shouting. Then silence.

Patrick, Mykle, Cameron, and I stand by the door. Everyone else is gone, except for Barry, who sits on the floor of his open cage rubbing his severed left knee and humming.

"Come on, Jeff," I say. "We have to go."

Jeff sits there a few moments squatting next to his sister, stroking her hair, not responding. I'm thinking he didn't hear me and I'm about to say it again, when he looks at us.

"You guys go ahead," he says. "I think I'll stay here."

"You know what they'll do to you," I say.

Jeff nods. "I can't leave her alone. She's my sister. I'm the reason she's here."

"Is there something we can do to help?" says Mykle.

"Nah. You need to take care of yourselves." Jeff offers a small smile. "Now get outta here. And Cam, try not to be such a fuckin' worrywart."

TWENTY-EIGHT

Out in the hallway there's not a soul, undead or alive. Other than the shouting and gunshot I heard earlier, there hasn't been a sound.

"Where is everyone?" says Mykle.

I shake my head. I'm guessing the other zombies have all gone down the stairs and are making their second run for freedom in as many days. Hopefully some of them will manage to get away this time.

The fact that it's been less than thirty-six hours since I last made this trip seems impossible. If I packed this much excitement into every day, I'd be worn out.

At least I'm making the most of my undeath.

We run past the first hallway junction and I look for the twins but don't see any sign of them. We don't have time to send out a search party, so I just have to hope that they know what they're doing.

We're approaching the second junction, with the exit door thirty feet beyond that, when we hear the sound of footsteps. Seconds later, the bald woman appears in the hallway ahead of us, accompanied by the rump roast who bumped into me at Rite Aid, both of them holding stun batons.

That's when I realize I left my stun baton in the kennel. So much for being prepared.

"Hey, here comes Santa Clauses," says the rump roast. "And a naked guy with barbecued legs. Now that's an image I could have lived without."

I look at the bald woman, who gives me this blank stare as if we never shared a moment. I don't know if she's on my side or just playing hard to get, but before I have a chance to say anything, I hear the sound of applause behind us. When I turn around, I see Ramirez holding a stun baton and the man with the 1970s porn star mustache walking toward us, clapping.

"Congratulations," he says, clapping three more times. "You're the first Reanimant to ever successfully break *into* a research facility. And I see you've brought some friends. How accommodating. That will make up for some of the ones you helped to escape."

"Who the hell are you?" I say.

He stops walking, the smile beneath his mustache faltering. I'm guessing he's not used to having zombies talk back.

"I'm your maker," he says. "The only reason you're even allowed to exist is because of me."

Mykle snorts. "Sounds like someone has delusions of splendor."

"I think you mean grandeur," says Cameron.

"Really?" says Mykle. "Even now?"

"Okay," says the porn star, who nods at Ramirez, the bald woman, and the rump roast. "What are you waiting for? Round them up."

The three of them start to close in on us. I don't know if it's going to do any good, but I put the thumb and index finger of my right hand in my mouth and let out a loud whistle. Everyone stops and I can see the doubt on the faces of Ramirez and the porn star, then I turn around and see the bald woman and the rump roast looking around. When nothing happens, the rump roast smiles and continues walking toward us.

"Nice try," he says. "But if there were more of . . ."

The bald woman jams her stun baton into the back of the rump roast and his words cut off as he spasms several times before collapsing face-first on the floor.

"What the hell are you doing?!" shouts the porn star.

The next moment, Zack and Luke come running around the corner behind him and reach the porn star and Ramirez before either of them has a chance to react. Needless to say there's a lot of shouting and blood, but to be fair there's more of the latter.

All of the blood and gore starts to make me gag again, so I turn around and see the bald woman staring at the carnage, her eyes wide and her face pale. I can see she's struggling with the scene that's playing out. After all, it's not every day you see two grown men torn apart by zombies. Unless, of course, you're a zombie. Then it's pretty much business as usual.

She blinks her eyes several times, then appears to force herself to focus on me.

"Here," she says, and holds out a set of keys, her hand shaking.

"What are these for?" I say.

"The body farm. They won't be looking for you in there."

I nod. "What's your name?"

She looks at me and offers a quizzical smile. "Shannon."

"Thank you, Shannon," I say. "For everything."

She gives me an odd look, one I'm not sure I can figure out. Maybe it's just my ego talking, but I think she kind of digs me. Then she turns and runs off down the hallway. I pick up the rump roast's stun baton. He's out cold from the fall but I zap him once more for being rude at the Rite Aid, then I whistle for Zack and Luke and lead my ragtag band of zombies out the exit and down the stairs.

When we get outside, the sun has nearly set and the lights have come on in the parking lot, illuminating the snow that's drifting down from the sky. The six of us run over to the ten-foot-tall wooden gate topped with razor wire and I fumble with the keys before Mykle points out that the gate is already unlocked.

Once we're all inside I close the gate, though we can't lock it, which I'm hoping won't be a problem. Just inside the gate are two old-fashioned metal mailboxes on posts. Zack and Luke investigate and find a box of green rubber surgical gloves in each mailbox. So, naturally, they both take out a pair and put them on.

"Now what?" says Cameron.

"It's a body farm," I say. "Let's make ourselves at home."

We all start walking up the path that leads past a variety of decomposing cadavers in various stages of decay, a few of them fully clothed but most of them naked, so Patrick is in good company.

Underneath the scent of pine trees and dead leaves is a sweet smell. Not like lavender or lilac or a tray of freshly baked chocolate chip cookies, but more like a truckload of peaches left out for a week in the hot sun and sprinkled with decaying fish. So it's not something you want to dab behind your ears.

The farther up the hillside we go, the more bodies we come across that are bloated and decomposing and turning into compost. With so many corpses melting out onto the ground, I'm guessing you need to watch where you step so you don't end up tracking anything out of here on your shoes.

"Oh great."

I look over and see Patrick making a face and looking at the bottom of his left foot.

We're about halfway up the hill, high enough so that we can see into the parking lot of the research facility with OHSU and the lights of Portland beyond it, when someone says, "Don't come any closer or I'll shoot."

In front of us stands one of the Breather Santas that was in the observation room, the one who had to take a leak. Either Matt or Brad, I don't know which. To be honest, when you get down to it, all Breathers kind of look alike. But he has a gun, which he's pointing at me, so that makes him stand out.

"What are you doing here?" I say, then look at Zack and Luke, who both shrug.

"I . . ." says the Breather, pointing his gun at Zack and Luke. "They . . ."

"Relax," I say. "No one's going to hurt you."

To be honest, I don't know if that's true. But it sounds good.

So he explains.

After Zack and Luke killed and partially ate the security guard, they ran off, leaving the two Breather Santas behind. Turns out the security guard didn't agree with the twins and they had to go find a bathroom. Which is what took them so long.

After the twins left, Matt/Brad grabbed the security guard's gun and went looking for help, but he went the wrong way. The next thing he knew, there were all of these zombies coming down the hallway, so he fired off a shot and then ran out of the building and down the stairs. When he found the gate to the body farm unlocked he ran inside and hid until he heard us coming after him.

"We weren't coming after you," I say. "We were—"

"You're a zombie, aren't you?" he says. "Jesus Christ, you're all zombies!"

I nod. "And there are six of us and only one of you, so you might want to reconsider your options."

"I know all about zombies," he says. "I've seen *Shaun*

of the Dead and *Zombieland,* so I know how to kill zombies. All I have to do is shoot you in the head."

"You know you shouldn't believe everything you see in the movies," I say.

Zack and Luke start to move around to flanking positions as Cameron and Mykle keep their distance. Patrick, meanwhile, continues to clean cadaver mud off the bottom of his foot.

"Now why don't you do everyone a favor and just go home before anyone gets hurt?" I say.

And by anyone, I mean him.

"I mean it!" he says, holding the gun up in front of him for emphasis and waving it back and forth. "I'll shoot you!"

Getting shot is the last thing I want. Healing from gunshot wounds takes longer than most other injuries. And since I can't eat Breather and I'm not getting my twice daily fix from the research facility anymore, I'm hoping we can avoid any unnecessary trauma.

But with the way his hand is shaking, I doubt I have much to worry about. If he hits me it'll likely be in the chest or an arm. Most likely, he'll miss me completely. The chances that he'll hit me in the head are about as good as someone making my story into a movie.

"Listen," I say . . .

Then he pulls the trigger and the world cuts to black.

TWENTY-NINE

I'm standing in the body farm with the snow falling around me and Zack and Luke having an early evening snack while Mykle and Cameron and Patrick walk around a clearing of bodies staked to the ground.

I look down at the face of the Santa Claus the twins are eating and recognize him. Matt or Brad, one of the two. Doesn't matter. I tried to tell him I didn't want anyone to get hurt, that he should leave while he had the chance, but Breathers can be pigheaded sometimes.

As I watch Zack and Luke devour Matt/Brad, it occurs to me that I'm not experiencing any nausea while they each start chewing on a different end of his intestines in a *Lady and the Tramp* spaghetti-and-meatball-scene kind of way. The fact that I can think this makes me wonder if something happened when I got shot in the head. Maybe whatever aversion to eating Breather had been instilled in me was blown out the back of my skull along with most of my gray matter.

I don't know how these things work, but it's the only explanation that makes any sense, so I'm going with it.

I'm tempted to join in and take a bite of Matt/Brad to test out my theory, but I decide I don't want to push it. The best course of action would probably be to take it slow. Baby steps. Though I probably don't want to wait too long since it's going to be tough to pass for a Breather when I have a gaping hole in the back of my head.

I leave Zack and Luke to their Breather banquet and head over to join the others.

"You're awake," says Patrick.

"How long was I out?" I ask.

"Not long," says Cameron. "Twenty minutes, tops."

I reach around and finger the back of my head and pull a piece of skull out of my hair. I can tell this is going to be messy.

"Can I see?" says Mykle.

He goes around behind me with the others to take a look and they all *ooh* and *ahh*. I don't mind the attention but I wish one of them had some Advil.

I point to the naked bodies staked down to the ground. "Some of our less fortunate friends?"

Cameron nods. "We've been looking for survivors, but we haven't found any. Everyone here seems to be gone."

Patrick walks around, looking for anyone who might still be conscious, apparently having made peace with the cadaver mud. Even if there were any survivors, the only humane thing to do would be to put them out of their misery.

"Any action from below?" I ask.

"We heard some voices and shouting about ten minutes ago," says Mykle, "but they all took off into the woods. No one came this way."

"All right then," I say. "I think we should probably hide out here for a few hours until things have calmed down. Maybe wait until midnight. Then make our way back to Zack and Luke's to get a change of clothes, grab anything useful, and get the hell out of town."

"Works for me," says Mykle.

"Me too," says Patrick.

I expect Cameron to be worried about the front gate being unlocked or that someone will find us if we stay here, but he's apparently taking Jeff's parting words to heart.

"Sounds like a good plan," he says.

So we sit and we wait and everyone shares in the holiday feast of Matt/Brad. I'm hesitant to dig in, mostly because if I'm wrong about my ability to eat Breather then I won't have much of a future and I'm not sure I'm ready to face that truth. Plus I prefer my Breather cooked medium. But when I take a small bite and discover that I can keep it down, I help myself to just enough flesh and internal organs so that I feel satisfied. That's the key to avoiding an upset stomach when eating Breather. Small portions.

The others all dig into their meal with enthusiasm. But unlike Hollywood zombies, who lack social etiquette and are short on table manners, there's not any growling or fighting. It's a lot more civilized. Kind of like the difference between a dinner party hosted by Hannibal Lecter and one hosted by Martha Stewart.

When it seems like it's late enough, we make our way down the hill and out of the body farm. Patrick suggests we cut down on the travel time and the chances of getting caught by stealing some wheels, since no one's going to be looking for a car full of zombies. So we find an older model black Toyota 4Runner, one that has a Hide-A-Key inside the left front wheel well, and all climb inside.

Cameron drives since he looks the most alive and because he knows his way around. Plus he wore a T-shirt under his Santa costume so he doesn't look like an escaped zombie Santa. Mykle rides shotgun, while Patrick and I sit in the backseat and the twins crawl into the rear storage area.

As Cameron drives off and starts making his way along the backstreets to Zack and Luke's, I look back at the twins, Santa's little helpers with their gloves and chins and turtlenecks covered in gore, and I get an idea.

I lean forward and say, "Can we make another pit stop?"

THIRTY

"**H**o ho ho," I say. "Wakey, wakey."

Annie's mother sits up in bed, her voice slurred and with a trace of panic. But mostly slurred. "What? Who . . . Who's there?"

"I'll give you three guesses," I say. "But the first two don't count."

From the chair next to her bed I turn on the bedside lamp, causing her to cover her eyes and squint. She looks at me, her eyes blinking. I watch her for any sign that she might start screaming, but she looks too drunk to be scared.

"Santa Claus?" she says.

"The one and only."

She swivels her head to look at Zack and Luke standing at the foot of her bed. "Who are they?"

"What do they look like?"

She looks them up and down for several moments before answering. "Really big elves."

"Right you are. Now we're all on the same page."

"What's that on their faces?" she asks. "Have they been eating strawberry pie?"

"Not exactly."

She looks around the bedroom and lets out a drunken little laugh. "I must be dreaming because this is just too weird to be real."

"Oh, it's real."

"I don't believe it." Her words come out slurred, the letters running together.

"Zack?"

Zack bends down and picks up a bucket full of ice water and throws it in the face of Annie's mother, who lets out a gasp of surprise and shock.

"Now that we've established that you're awake," I say, "let's set some rules."

"R-r-rules?" She sputters and gasps. "Wh-what are you talking about?"

She's still drunk, but at least she sounds more coherent.

"Your daughter," I say. "We're talking about Annie."

"Annie?" Her eyes grow wide. "Where is she? Is she okay? What have you done with her?"

"Annie's asleep in bed with visions of candy canes dancing in her head. You don't have to worry about her. You just have to worry about you."

"Me?"

"Yes, Lori. You."

"How do you kn-know my name?"

In truth, I got her name from her phone bill, but she doesn't need to know that.

"Because I'm Santa Claus," I say. "I have a list of all the good little boys and girls. And the bad ones. And you, Lori Walker, have been a *very* bad little girl."

She looks at me, her shirt drenched with ice water and her eyes wide. Then she looks at Zack and Luke, who respond with matching smiles and sit down on the edge of her bed.

She scoots away from them. "What have I d-d-done?"

"What have you done?" I start counting off the reasons on my fingers. "You drink. You stay out late. You neglect your daughter. Should I keep going?"

She opens her mouth to offer up a rebuttal, but I hold up my hand and she stops.

"In short, you, Lori Walker, are a horrible excuse for a mother."

She looks from me to the twins, who both nod at her in perfect sync.

"Wh-wh-what do you want me t-t-to do?"

"Do you know what Annie told me she wanted for Christmas?" I say. "What she wanted more than anything else in the world?"

She shakes her head.

"She wished you would spend more time with her."

She looks at me, blinking several times and not saying a word, before she lets out something that sounds like a tiny little sob.

"So first of all, you need to start spending more time with Annie instead of going out and doing whatever it is you're doing."

I realize Santa should be more specific about her

activities, but I hope she's too freaked out to call me on my lack of detail.

"Second, you're going to join AA," I say. "Get a sponsor. Sober up. You can't be a good mother and spend quality time with your daughter if you're drunk. Plus it sets a bad example."

She nods several times, short and quick.

From her bedside table I pick up an ashtray overflowing with dead cigarettes.

"And finally, you need to stop smoking. Secondhand smoke is bad for children. Do you want to be responsible for giving your daughter lung cancer?"

She shakes her head.

"Good," I say, and set the ashtray back down. "Now there's one more matter we need to clear up."

"What's th-that?"

I lean forward and point to the bullet hole in my forehead. "Do you know what that is, Lori?"

She leans forward to get a better look, then pulls back and shakes her head.

"That's where someone shot me." I turn around to show her the back of my head. "And that's where the bullet came out."

She chokes back either a gag or a scream, I can't tell which.

"And what you thought was strawberry pie stains on my elves?" I say, turning back to her. "That's blood. Human blood."

She looks at Zack and Luke, her lips attempting to form words but nothing's coming out.

"So be good, Lori. Because I know when you've been sleeping and I know when you're awake. I know when you've been bad or good, so be good for Annie's sake. Otherwise I'm going to have to send my elves for a little follow-up to make sure you behave."

Zack and Luke both smile at her and lick their lips at the same time.

"Do we understand one another?" I say.

She nods.

"You're going to be a good mother to Annie from now on?"

She nods again.

"And you're going to make sure she gets everything she wants for Christmas?"

"Yes." The word comes out barely more than a whisper.

"That's a good girl." I nod to Zack and Luke, who get up from her bed and grab her cordless telephone and cell phone before they walk out of the room. I follow along behind them, leaving the bedside light on, and turn around as I leave.

"Merry Christmas, Lori," I say. And then I close her bedroom door.

ONE
YEAR
LATER

"**A**nnie!"

Annie sits on the couch watching *Miracle on 34th Street*. The original one with Natalie Wood as Susan Walker and Maureen O'Hara as her mom. The remake is okay, but Annie thinks Edmund Gwenn is a better Kris Kringle.

"Annie!"

Her mother has been calling her for the past couple of minutes, but Annie is at the best part in the movie. Her favorite part, right near the end, when the lawyer proves that Kris Kringle is the real Santa Claus. She likes the lawyer, but she can't remember his real name.

"Annie!"

She waits until the scene is finished and claps the way she always does when the judge declares Kris Kringle the real Santa, then she hops up off the couch and runs down the hall to see what her mother can't find this time.

"There you are," says her mother, in black dress slacks and a black bra, searching through her closet as Annie appears in the bedroom doorway. "Why didn't you answer me?"

"I was watching *Miracle on 34th Street.*"

"Didn't you watch that yesterday?"

Annie shrugs. "I like watching it."

Her mother continues to look through the closet, chewing on her nicotine gum. She's been chewing it for the last year ever since she stopped smoking. She doesn't use it as much as she used to, but Annie notices that she's started chewing it more often the closer it gets to Christmas.

"Have you seen my black sweater, kiddo?"

"It's at the dry cleaners."

"Shit," says her mother, then looks at Annie. "Sorry about that."

"It's okay. I say 'shit,' too, sometimes."

Her mother gives her a smile, then walks over and ruffles Annie's hair before she starts looking through her closet again. Annie hates it when any of the annoying boys at school ruffle her hair. She knows that means they like her, but they're still annoying. But she doesn't mind when her mother does it.

"Why don't you wear your green turtleneck instead?" says Annie. "You look good in turtlenecks. Plus it's green. You know. Like Christmas."

Her mother reaches into the closet and pulls out the green turtleneck, holds it up, and lets out a little shiver, like she's cold. Then she puts the turtleneck back and pulls out a red sweater.

"How about this, instead?" she says, holding the sweater up in front of her.

Annie smiles and nods. "That's even better."

Her mother slips the sweater over her head, then looks at her watch. "I better get going."

Her mother hasn't been late for work in nearly a year.

Annie walks back out to the living room and looks at the Christmas tree standing in the corner near the front window, decorated with garlands and colored blinking lights that reflect off the red and silver and gold glass ornaments. Beneath the tree are half a dozen presents wrapped up in ribbons and bows, most of them for her. And on the wall next to the electric heater are stockings that say ANNIE and MOM.

Annie looks at the stockings and smiles when she thinks about last Christmas. Sometimes it doesn't seem like it was real, that she just imagined it all because she was unhappy. But then all she has to do is pull out her box with all of the stocking stuffers Santa brought her and she knows it really happened.

Her mother doesn't remember all of the Santas and the elves and how they brought a tree and decorations and a stocking for Annie. She doesn't even remember coming into Annie's room later that night and crawling into bed with her, wet and shaking and crying.

Or if she does, she never talks about it. So Annie never brings it up.

"How do I look?" says her mother, walking into the room and twirling around once like a supermodel.

"Awesome."

"There's meat loaf and mashed potatoes in the refrigerator from last night for lunch," says her mother as she grabs her raincoat by the front door. "And some asparagus."

"Yuck."

"I know it's not your favorite, but try to eat some for me, okay? And when I get home, we'll order pizza and then make Christmas cookies together. Deal?"

"Pepperoni pizza?"

"Whatever you want."

"Deal." Annie puts out her hand and they shake on it.

"Be good, kiddo," says her mother, ruffling Annie's hair again.

"I will. 'Cause Santa's watching. And he knows if you've been bad or good, so be good for goodness' sake. Right?"

Her mother's smile suddenly vanishes and her lips twitch several times. For a moment Annie thinks she's going to cry, then her mother composes herself and smiles again. "That's right, kiddo."

Annie smiles. "I love you, Mom."

Her mother kisses Annie on the cheek. "I love you, too."

Annie watches her mom walk out the door into the rain and waits until she drives off down the street. As soon as she's gone, Annie grabs some Famous Amos cookies and puts them into a Ziploc bag, then she slips on her galoshes and rain slicker and goes outside.

None of the kids at Annie's school and certainly none

of her friends believe in Santa Claus anymore. That sort of thing happens as you get older.

But Annie knows better.

Because she spent the day with Santa Claus last year, watching movies and drinking hot chocolate and making up a Christmas bedtime story. And because he brought her a stocking and a tree and a house full of decorations.

But more than anything, Annie believes in Santa because he gave her what she asked him for Christmas. Maybe it wasn't the big stuffed panda bear, but she got something way better. The thing she wanted most of all.

Annie walks up the hill past the homes decorated for Christmas, but she isn't interested in them. She's gone up to the house at the top of the hill almost every day for the past week to visit Santa Claus, hoping she can bring him to life the same way she did last year, but so far she hasn't had any luck.

She reaches the house, decorated with all of the elves and reindeer and the life-size Santa sitting on the front porch. Annie looks around to make sure no one's watching, then she goes through the gate and up to the porch and stands in front of Santa.

"I'm back again," she says, then pulls the Ziploc bag out of her pocket and sets it in his lap. "And I brought you some more cookies, too."

Santa just sits there, staring at her with his blank expression.

Annie reaches over and removes the hat from his head and regards the mannequin with the fake white wig and beard. It doesn't look anything like the real Santa, and she knows this probably won't work because it hasn't worked so far, but she has to try.

She puts the hat on his head and steps back, then adjusts it, making sure to do it the same way she did that first time a year ago, but nothing happens.

It's just a fake Santa with a fake beard and nothing more.

Annie stands there a few moments longer, then she sighs and turns and walks away, leaving the cookies for whoever wants to eat them.

When Annie gets back home, she makes herself some hot chocolate and sits down to watch the rest of *Miracle on 34th Street,* hoping that will help to cheer her up. She's just settling in when there's a knock at the front door, so she puts the movie on pause, gets off the couch, walks over to the window, and looks out through the blinds, but she doesn't see anyone. She figures it's just some stupid kids playing doorbell ditch, and opens the front door to yell at them.

Instead, sitting there on the front stoop is a big box wrapped in gold paper with a gold bow. A card on the top of the box declares:

TO: ANNIE

Annie steps out onto the stoop and looks to see if whoever left the present is still around. But she doesn't see anyone. Just a red sport utility vehicle that pulls away from the curb and drives off down the street.

She looks around one last time, then picks up the box that comes up past her waist and closes the door.

She sets the present on the floor next to the coffee table, wondering what could be inside. She knows it's not Christmas yet, and that she should probably wait to open her gift, but she can't stand not knowing. Besides, it's so big.

So she opens it.

Inside is a big stuffed panda bear, soft and cuddly, with a small envelope taped to the bear, addressed to her.

There's a note inside the envelope that says:

Dear Annie,

Thank you again for the movies and hot chocolate. Merry Christmas.

Love, Santa

P.S. Tell your mother she's been a good little girl.

"If I Only Had Some Brains"
lyrics by Andy Warner

I could gnaw away the hours
Delightfully devour
Digesting Johns and Janes
And my mouth I'd be fillin'
While my hands were busy killin'
If I only had some brains

I'd faddle and I'd fiddle
Fat fry you on the griddle
Sautéing your remains
On your flesh I'd be snackin'
And your skull I would be crackin'
If I only had some brains

Oh, ever since I've died
I've longed for blood and gore
Just to sit and eat the brains that I adore
And then I'd sit and eat some more

I would bake you in a muffin
Complete you with some stuffin'
Or maybe some whole grains
In a shake made with dairy
I would top you with a cherry
If I only had some brains

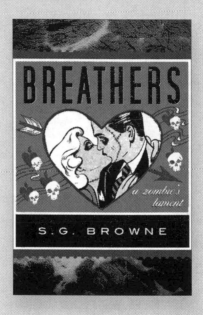

Printed in the United States
By Bookmasters